Free Use Wedding Series

Lacey Cross

Twisted Rose Publishing

CONTENTS

Taking Them All	1
Chapter 1	3
Chapter 2	15
Borrowing the Bride	21
Chapter 1	23
Chapter 2	31
Chapter 3	35
Pleasing The Crowd	47
Chapter 1	49
Chapter 2	57
Chapter 3	63
Gratifying the Guys	73
Chapter 1	75
Chapter 2	83
Chapter 3	89

Chapter 4   99

Auditioning The Band   111

Chapter 1   113

Chapter 2   121

Chapter 3   127

Chapter 4   139

Acknowledgments   143

About Lacey Cross   145

Taking Them All

CHAPTER 1

My husband, Jonas, and I have an agreement that I can fuck whoever I want, whenever, as long as I come home and give him all the juicy details. So when one of my best friends invites me to her second bachelorette party at a ski lodge in the mountains, I'm not that excited since I don't like to ski. But it's whatever, I'm sure I can find a little action over the weekend. Some lonely guy who fancies cuddling up by the fire in his room and slipping his cock inside me while the snow drifts against the window. Then I'll come home to Jonas, and he'll fuck me as I tell him all the filthy things I did over the weekend.

Sighing, I watch Vanessa, the bride-to-be, teeter off into the bedroom after a long gab session between the four of us who came on the trip. Our cabin has one bedroom with two sets of bunk beds, and Vanessa and I are the last ones left awake.

Right before she closes the bedroom door, she slurs, "Goodnight, Nadia," and I softly call out goodnight. Not that the others are going to wake up with how much booze they downed.

I'm the only one who didn't drink, so I'm wide awake at midnight. Scanning the room, I snicker at how we trashed the place in just a few hours. The cabin is decorated with sturdy, rustic furniture, and it was immaculate when we got here. Now it's littered with empty Champagne bottles and streamers from party poppers. I could be nice and clean up for everyone, but, nah, they can help me in the morning.

I didn't realize that the lodge was only going to have individual cabins. There's no common room or bar for me to meet a random older gentleman who knows how to treat a woman right. Not being able to find a guy to hook up with annoys my buzzing pussy. Man, I shaved and everything for this trip. What a waste. I'm not sure I would have come if I had known I was going to be trapped in a cabin for the weekend. I'm not going skiing with them tomorrow, so what am I even doing here?

This weekend getaway was a last-minute decision, so not all of the bridesmaids are here. Vanessa requested one last trip as a single woman and tossed the plan together. I could have said I was busy, but my slutty pussy thought she was going to get sex, so I said yes.

I slip my hands down the front of my tiny, cotton shorts and panties and rub my pussy. Vanessa was half passed out, so she's probably already asleep, and the other two went to bed hours ago. They didn't wake up when Vanessa was singing at the top of her lungs, so I know a little moaning from me won't disturb them.

Dipping my finger into my wet pussy, I gather the moisture to use as lubrication against my clit. The wooden chair isn't comfortable, but it'll have to do. I scoot my ass to the edge and rest my head on the back of the chair so I can close my eyes and go to town on my clit. My moans aren't quiet as I caress my clit in circles. Each brush of my finger creeps me closer to my orgasm, and I daydream that my husband is on his knees between my legs, licking my clit and fingering me. I know what I'm asking for when I get home. I'll tell him it was a waste of a trip and I deserve a good pussy licking.

My thigh muscles tense, and I arch my back as the pleasure builds. I'm breathing in quick puffs and continuous moans. When I speed up my rubbing, it tips me over the edge. I gasp as the waves of bliss wash over me, but it's a tiny orgasm and the peak is short-lived. Ugh, a powerful orgasm would have made me sleepy and instead I'm even more awake.

Pulling my hands from my shorts, I wipe my fingers on the fabric and sigh. If I were at home, my husband would take care of my neediness. He's always good about that, and I love him dearly. We have a great sex life. If he wasn't so hot for me to sleep with other guys and tell him about it, I wouldn't do it. Don't get me wrong, I have fun, but I'd never cheat on my husband. But he loves it, and the rough fucking he always gives me after I describe blowing some other guy, or how my pussy was pounded so hard I saw stars, is fabulous.

The small living room is sweltering from the dying embers in the log fireplace. It was warm before my orgasm and now I'm sweaty and miserable. I flutter the edge of my tank top, so it billows out and creates a tiny breeze, but it doesn't help. Shit, I need to cool down.

Getting up, I step outside the cabin and the door gently clicks shut behind me. I groan happily at the slap of icy wind. I'm only going to be out here for a few more seconds, which is good since I'm standing on a small wooden porch in my bare feet, tiny shorts, and tank top. Once I cool down, I'll welcome the warmth of the room.

The lodge has six cabins, all close together, and four of them have no lights on. But the one directly across from me looks like a party cabin. The lights are blazing, and 90s rock music blasts through an open window. Thankfully, we couldn't hear the music through the thick walls of our cabin. The noise level reminds me of college and the parties I attended at the frat houses. I wish the people in the cabin well, whatever they're celebrating, but I have to get inside before I freeze to death.

When I grip the doorknob, it doesn't turn. Staring at the door in disbelief, I take a few seconds to comprehend that I'm locked out. OH FUCK.

I beat on the door frantically. Vanessa better open this door right quick. I shouldn't have even come outside in this outfit. The icy wood against my feet makes me bang harder on the door. I stop knocking and try to listen to see if I can hear any movement, but the thick walls and door prevent me from being able to tell. Wait, how long does it take for someone to freeze to death?

I curl my toes, and I can already tell they're too cold. Maybe if I knock long enough, Vanessa will open the door. But will it be before I lose anything to frostbite? It only takes me a split second to decide what to do. Before I give it too much thought, I'm dashing down the snowy walkway, straight for the party cabin. The snow has been falling for hours and the untouched path makes it easy to keep my footing. My bare feet sink into the fluffy whiteness as I speed walk as quickly as possible while still being careful not to trip.

Stumbling up the porch, I bang on the cabin door, and it's almost immediately answered.

A massive, ginger-haired guy with a beard blinks at me before calling over his shoulder, "Hey, who hired a stripper to come all the way up here?"

I open my mouth to tell him I'm not a freaking stripper when he grips my shoulder and tugs me into the cabin. "Come inside. You're crazy to be standing out there without shoes on and in that skimpy outfit."

The warmth of the room smacks me in the face, and I almost sigh in happiness. Oh, thank God. Ginger Man, as I've now dubbed him, draws me to the couch in front of the fireplace, pushes me down, and sits beside me. He pulls my feet into his lap and rubs them between his warm hands.

My red toenails and lightly tanned skin contrast against his ivory tone. His hands are enormous and make my tiny feet appear even smaller. The longer he rubs them, the more it's like a foot massage. I close my eyes, sink into the couch cushions, and moan softly. Keeping my eyes closed, I enjoy the massage while my other senses take over. Someone turned down the music, and the hum of voices tells me there are several people here–at least five, maybe more. There's enough talking that I can't hear everything going on at once, and I have to concentrate to isolate the voices. Clearly, there's a card game going on, since every few seconds a table gets thumped, people laugh, and other people groan. Another group of guys is close by, discussing time travel theory.

"So, who ordered the stripper?" Ginger Man calls out again, and a chorus of "Not me" and "I don't know" rings out.

"Maybe it was Ron?" a deep voice suggests, and a bunch of people agree that it sounds like something Ron would do.

Wait, are they all men? I open my eyes, peek over the side of the couch, and count ten guys with a quick glance. I snuggle back down on the couch and watch Ginger Man rubbing my feet.

Hey, this guy is pretty damn sexy. I've always had a thing for bigger men because I love feeling small and helpless when they pin me down. Add in the red hair and beard, and I'm sold. My pussy flutters and reminds me that my last orgasm wasn't the best.

"So..." Ginger Man smiles at me. "Are you going to strip for us?"

His hands turn into more of a caress, and I almost groan at how erotic it feels. Here I was, wishing I could find a guy to fuck tonight, and the universe handed me more men than I can handle...

Or did it?

My body zings alive, and my nipples pucker as I imagine fucking multiple men tonight. Can I really do this? My husband said whoever, whenever. A splash of wetness leaks from my pussy. Oh, hell yeah, let's do this. It's going to be the sluttiest thing I've ever done in my life, but I'm going to fuck them all.

I remove my feet from his hands and curl them under me as I shift onto my knees. Smiling seductively, I purr at Ginger Man, "Ron didn't hire a stripper..." I don't actually know who this Ron person is, but I go with it and continue, "Ron hired a freeuse slut for anyone to use."

My voice was loud enough that the guys discussing time travel stopped talking. "Well, holy fuck," one of them murmurs.

"Me first!" chimes in a second guy, and a thrill runs through me, straight to my clit.

I'm already breathing heavily, and my tingling pussy makes me yearn to straddle Ginger Man and grind against him. Ginger Man stares at me for a few seconds, and a ball of lust lodges in my gut while my breasts ache to be touched. Someone argues in the background about deserving to be first.

"Shut up!" Ginger Man bellows, and the entire room quiets. "I'm first," he states in a tone that leaves no room for disagreement.

Several people murmur in approval, and longing blossoms in my core. I'm not sure I've ever desired to be fucked as much as I need this guy to fuck me right now. Is he going to take me to the back room? This cabin is larger than the one I'm in and has several doors leading to other rooms. We could go into a bedroom, and the guys could come in one at a time.

"Get on your hands and knees," Ginger Man commands.

My eyes widen. Uh... I open my mouth to protest, and he gives me a wicked smile. "You said Ron paid you to be a freeuse slut. Is there a problem?"

I close my mouth and shake my head. My entire body vibrates from sexual tension. Holy fuck, am I really going to do this? I stand up and sink to my knees on a fake sheepskin rug in front of the fireplace. When Ginger Man kneels behind me and tugs my shorts and panties down, excitement pulses through me and rushes straight to my shaved cunt. Looks like I really *am* going to do this.

He groans. "Look at that pretty pussy, you guys. All shaved and wet for us."

Oh fuck, that's hot. My mind blips out, and I shake my ass at him, daring him to fuck me. Instead of using his cock, he rubs my velvety folds with a finger and presses one inside my pussy. I moan at the invasion. God, his finger is thick. If that's one finger, what will his cock feel like?

He slips a second finger in, stretching me out even more, and I grind back against his hand. He laughs and finger fucks me slowly while lust almost overwhelms me. When he shoves in a third finger, I'm so amazingly full, I think I'm going to explode and come all over his hand, but I don't.

"Guys, she's so warm and tight. Do you think I should show her what my cock feels like?"

A chorus of guys call out "Yes" and "Do it," and knowing there are men watching us is crazy hot. All I can see is the fireplace, and I'm afraid to peek behind me. I might freeze up with a ton of eyes staring at me. It's better to imagine it. I assume it's true, but I don't know for a fact.

Clothes rustle behind me and then the tip of a cock rubs up and down my slit. The head is thick and bulbous, and I bet his shaft is huge. He grabs onto my hip with one massive hand and steadies me while he presses his cock against my entrance.

"You ready for this, slut?" he growls.

I squeal as he applies pressure. As the head slips in, it stretches me out. "Ohhh god, yes," I moan, and he plunges straight to my core with no further warning.

"Fuuuuuck!" I cry out from the exquisite pleasure that borders on pain because of how enormous he is.

Holy hell. I knew he'd be big, but I wasn't expecting THIS big. My head whirls as he pummels into my pussy.

His voice is almost jolly when he talks to the room. "You know what the best thing about a freeuse slut is, boys?"

Someone asks him, "What?" and he whacks against my cunt so vigorously, his balls slap against my clit.

"Fuck!" I can't hold back, and I'm swearing with each thrust.

"You can use her, and you don't have to wait for her to come."

Ugh, what? My pussy clenches around him and I'm so close to coming that I consider begging. He gives a loud grunt, and I can tell he's about to erupt. His shaft pulsates, and he clasps my waist with both hands and yanks me against him, grinding his cock deep inside. His head rubs my magical spot, and with a few brushes of the tip, I explode.

"Ohhhhh fuuuuuuucck," I scream as he blows his load inside my pussy, and waves of rapture overwhelm me. His cock jerks and his hot cum paints my inner walls. He pulls out with a loud, wet sound and his seed gushes out and drips down my thighs.

Leaning my head down on my forearms with my ass in the air, I try to catch my breath as aftershocks of pleasure ripple through my core. I'm not paying attention until another cock probes my slickness.

Oh, shit. I'm not sure what I was expecting, but someone replacing Ginger Man immediately wasn't a thought. The next dude slams into me and starts bulldozing my pussy.

"Hey, you're right," the dude fucking me states. "I can come whenever, and she won't complain."

I rest my face on my forearms, ready to grumble that I will complain, but the pleasure in my core builds again. Am I going to have another orgasm already? This guy's cock isn't as large, but he's enthusiastic and hitting a pleasant spot repeatedly.

Another climax builds, and right before I come, the dude fucking me spurts his load with a loud groan while the room cheers him on. How many of these guys are going to fuck me?

I don't even realize the guy left my ass until a strong spank makes me squeak, "Hey!"

"Get back up on all fours, slut," a deep voice commands, and I obey without question.

I gasp when another cock probes my sodden hole. This new guy fucks me slowly. I wasn't expecting gentleness, and the pleasure is more intense because I can feel every one of his long strokes.

"I hope Ron paid well. You're going to be used all night long," he declares, and the zing of delight from his words almost tips me over the edge again. Oh, fuck. ALL night? Am I up for this?

He gives a few experimental strong whacks against my pussy, and I cry out from the sharp pleasure. Jesus Christ, I'm about to come again. A warm glow envelops me, and my brain gets fuzzy. Each stroke is better than the last, and I'm floating in a place where time doesn't matter.

The guy clutches my long brown hair in his fist and pulls my head back while he drills into me, hard and deep.

"Come for me," he demands, and my body obeys with no thought.

I cry out as my third orgasm of the night hits me like a train wreck, and I convulse around his cock. He spanks me again, and I collapse onto my arms as he yells like he scored a goal with his orgasm. My entire body vibrates, and my pussy flutters as more cum coats my walls. When he pulls out, our combined juices rush down my leg.

I'm a mess, and I barely notice the next guy press into my pussy. I lose count of the men who fuck me, and I don't know how many orgasms I have after my sixth. It's a stream of pleasure, each orgasm building on the last. At some point, a guy decides to fuck my mouth, and it's the first time I get to see who's connected to the cocks. This guy is average looking, but his cock isn't. He's got a thick, meaty shaft, and I lick my lips eagerly.

As he eases his cock down my throat, I taste myself on him, so I know he's already fucked me. He uses my mouth while another guy drills into my pussy, and his shaft muffles my moans. He blows his load sooner than I expect, and I'm not able to swallow it fast enough. Cum and spit drip down my chin when he removes himself from my mouth, and he's immediately replaced with another guy.

On and on it goes. Once that first guy realized they could get a blowjob, the rest join in and go for round two with my mouth. I welcome each one and suck on them greedily. I can tell they all fucked me because I'm cleaning my juices off their cocks. The guys pounding behind me create a nice back-and-forth movement between me and the cocks in my mouth, and each whack against my sodden hole shoves the cocks deeper down my throat. My screams of pleasure when I orgasm are stifled, and all I hear now is the crackling of the fire, cheering from everyone as they watch, and the groans and moans of various men as they fuck me with abandon.

I'm lost in a haze of desire, and I don't know how many cocks I suck. Each one is different: thick, slim, short, cut, uncut. After so many in a row, they all blend together. I don't even have time to wipe the cum off my face, and some of the men grip my head and smear jizz up into my hairline. This is, by far, the filthiest thing I've done in my entire life, and I'm eager to get home and tell my husband and get my reward for being such a slut.

Eventually, I'm flipped over, and a gigantic body covers me while an enormous cock slides into my sore pussy. It's Ginger Man again, and he fucks me slowly while kissing me. Our tongues swirl together, and I cling to his massive shoulders. My pussy squeezes around him, tiny aftershocks from all my orgasms. His breath is ragged as we rock together.

"Do you need more cum?" he groans.

All I can do is murmur, "Please."

He kisses me again as his cock pulsates and fills me. My pussy clenches, and another soft climax runs through me, gentle waves after so many sharp peaks. He fucks me through my orgasm, and when he finally pulls out, the room is silent.

Sudden cheering and the chorus of claps make me smile dreamily. Jesus, my hubby is going to love this story.

Ginger Man helps me stand, pulls my panties and shorts back up for me, and leads me to the couch. Someone brings me a bottle of water, and another person hands me a thick wad of cash. The room is still spinning, and I'm uncertain what this is for. I glance at Ginger Man with the question in my eyes, and he grins at me.

"It's your tip."

I try to hand it back to him. I don't want their money, and since I'm not really a stripper, I wasn't thinking about a tip. He takes it back, and instead of setting it aside, he shoves it down the front of my shorts and grins at me.

"Keep it. I insist."

A strong rap on the door makes everyone jump, and one man opens it. Vanessa is standing there.

"Have you guys seen…" She spots me sitting on the couch and her eyes widen.

I can guess how filthy and used I look, but I don't care.

"Hi." I wave at her weakly, and Ginger Man guides me to the door.

Everyone says goodbye, and some praise me and say they had a fabulous time. Ginger Man hands me an enormous pair of men's slippers to wear home, and I promise to leave them on the porch in the morning. Vanessa is silent as she helps me back to our cabin. When we walk in, I turn to her. She looks like she's going to say something, but I hold up my hand.

"I must sleep. We'll talk later."

She nods, and I stumble into the bedroom and launch myself onto the lower bunk. When my husband said whoever, whenever… I hope he meant ten guys. I fall asleep with a smile on my face.

Chapter 2

The next morning, while the other bridesmaids are outside playing in the snow, I tell Vanessa the story. Her shock and delight have me going into great detail, and I swear her to secrecy. The rest of the weekend, I feel her eyes on me, and I catch her staring toward the men's cabin with a pensive look. I'm not sure what she's thinking, but I can tell it's not directed at me, so I don't let it concern me much. I'm too worked up and excited about seeing my husband soon, and I daydream about what will happen since I'm not totally sure what to expect. He'll probably be shocked, like Vanessa, and then horny... or at least I hope that's how it goes.

I want to return the slippers to the guys and sneakily give them their cash back before we leave the lodge. It felt dishonest for me to keep the tip money. I worked hard for them, but their hot, sticky cum was enough payment. I tuck the money into the toe of one slipper and put them in a plastic bag. Creeping over to their cabin, I leave the bag on the porch for them to find later.

I don't get home until Monday afternoon while my husband is at work, and I text him to let him know I'm back. I'm already wet and greedy for his cock. No matter how many other guys I fuck, my husband is my rock, and nothing compares to the love I feel when he fills me with his seed and leaves me with a gushing creampie.

Nadia: I'm home!

Jonas: I can't wait to see you, baby. I hope you had a fun trip.

I giggle as I type.

Nadia: I have a story for you. I exercised my "anyone, anywhere" free pass.

Jonas: Oh, really? I'm intrigued. Tell me more.

Hmm, what should I tell him? Nope, I'm making him wait.

Nadia: You don't get the story until you're home and inside me. But I'll tell you a tidbit. It involved more than one cock.

He takes a while to reply. Work must be busy.

Jonas: OK, baby, but I expect you naked and in bed when I get home.

Ohhh, heck yeah.

Nadia: Yes, sir!

I don't normally call him 'sir,' so I send him a winking emoji along with the message. He replies with a GIF of a teddy bear blowing me kisses.

Sighing happily, I glance at the clock on my phone. Ugh, there are still three hours until he gets off work. My pussy buzzes angrily. Yeah, it's going to be a long afternoon.

I'm naked and lying on top of the covers when he walks into the bedroom after work. I couldn't wait, and I rubbed my clit a little in anticipation, forcing myself to stop when I got too close to coming. He'll be able to slide right inside me and fuck me hard. I'm more than ready for him.

Jonas grins when he sees me. "Good. You're right where I want you."

I pat the bed next to me. "Join me, and I'll tell you the story."

"Hold that thought. I'll be right back."

I pout as he leaves the bedroom, and my pussy quivers. I hear him go into the bathroom, but he doesn't take long. When he comes back, he's naked, and his thick cock juts straight out. I swear it gives me a little wave as he approaches the bed. Wetness leaks from my pussy, and I roll one of my nipples between my fingers while Jonas settles in next to me. I'm almost too turned on to tell him what happened. I long to climb on top of him and ride him until I cream all over his cock, but he deserves story time first.

He leans into me and softly brushes his lips against mine before applying pressure and coaxing them open. He tastes like coffee, and I groan as our tongues dance. His cock is heavy and thick as it presses against the softness of my tummy. I reach down to stroke him, and tendrils of delight light up my core the longer we kiss.

His cock is wet with pre-cum, and I use it as lubricant to slide my fingers firmly up and down his length. I take my time with it, so he doesn't get too excited. I'm vibrating with desire and desperate for him to fuck me, but I force myself to take things slow, so I don't deprive him of any pleasure.

He breaks off the kiss and nibbles down the column of my neck, heading straight for my tits. He starts with small kisses on my nipple for a moment before taking the entire tip into his mouth.

"Tell me what you did," he demands around my breast as he continues to suck and pull on my nipple.

Fuck, it's hard to think when he's doing that. Okay, focus, Nadia. I groan when he pinches the other nipple—hard.

Shiiit. Okay… Okay… must concentrate. Since he's teasing me, I'm going to turn the tables on him. "Guess how many guys I fucked this weekend?"

That makes him pause since he already knows it was more than one. "Uh… three?"

He goes back to sucking on my breast, and I giggle. "Higher."

He pulls back and stares at me. "Four?"

"Higher."

His eyes go round. "FIVE?"

"Higher." I give him a mysterious smile and tug on his cock.

His cock grows harder, and I feel a shiver run through his body. "Nadia, just tell me how many." His tone says he's done with our guessing game.

Kissing him briefly, I move my mouth to his ear and whisper. "I don't know, but I think it was ten. Sometimes I had two at once... and the rest would watch."

I lean back so I can see his face, trying to assess what he's thinking. A flicker of shock passes over him, but his eyes quickly turn feral.

"How many orgasms did you have?"

"Um... I lost count."

He crawls on top of me, tugging my legs open. I'm not fighting him. In fact, I help by spreading them as wide as I can. He fits the head of his cock against my pussy but doesn't sink in.

"Nadia, you know what happens when you fuck other guys, right?"

I nod. "Uh-huh, you get to use me and come as many times as I did. Without trying to make me come."

He flashes a wicked grin. "So should we call it ten orgasms?"

Oh, shit. Even if he fucked me twice per day, that means I'm not coming for almost a week. I use my cutest voice possible, the one I know he can't resist. "Um... I think it was six?"

He laughs. "You don't seem too sure of that number."

Thank God it's not how many times the men came since I believe most of them came twice: once in my pussy, and once in my mouth.

"No... no... I'm SURE it was six." I blink at him innocently and hope he buys my act.

"Hmm, okay... if you're sure."

"Oh, yes, I'm... fuuuuuuck." He slams into me, straight to my core, and a massive spike of pleasure rushes through me.

He whacks against me. "Nadia, you are a thirsty little cum slut."

"Oh, God. Yes, I am."

When he grabs my wrists and pins them above my head, I close my eyes and take my punishment. He whacks against me, and each thrust shoots spirals of bliss through my core. The rule is that if I come, fine, but he's not waiting for me. Chances are good I'm going to come at this rate.

He's panting, and his voice is rough. "Did you like fucking all those men?"

My clit throbs, and I need to come so badly. I cry out when he thrusts extra hard and whimper, "Yes, it felt so good."

"Did you think of me while they used you?"

Ohhh, there we go. Love for my husband floods through me. "Yes," I gasp as a zing of bliss almost makes me come. "I always think of you. Everything I do is for you."

He groans, lets go of my wrists, and pushes my knees up to my chest. "I'm going to fill you up and you're going to be dripping for days."

He jackhammers into me, and when he hits the perfect spot, my orgasm rips through me. I squeal and shudder while my pussy clenches around his cock. Knowing I came drives him into a frenzy, and he slams into me repeatedly.

He comes with a growl, and his cock spasms. "I love you," he groans as he shoots load after load of hot cum deep inside me. His body twitches against me, and he slows down his thrusts before withdrawing and lowering my legs. We're both in a daze as he collapses next to me and cuddles close.

My heart races, and it takes a while for my breathing to calm down. Our bodies are slick with sweat, but we don't move. He doesn't speak, and when I look at him, he's got a glazed, sexually satisfied glow.

This is how it always is after I've been with another guy. It's going to be several days of a gloriously possessive and insatiable husband, and it's why I enjoy being a hotwife. None of this would be fun without my husband. Sure, the sex is great. But while the men are fucking me, I think of how Jonas will react later, and it increases the pleasure in the moment. I always come harder knowing my husband is going to get a thrill from hearing about my slutty adventures.

After a bit, I can tell he's coming back to his senses because he caresses my hand and kisses my shoulder.

I turn my head to look at him and whisper, "I love you."

His eyes glint when he replies, "That's one."

Giggling, I give him a peck on the mouth. "Yep, five more to go."

It's going to be a fun few days at my house.

The End

BORROWING THE BRIDE

Chapter 1

We're not superstitious, so Mason and I didn't sleep separately the night before our wedding. When I wake up the morning of our big day, Mason is on his side, already awake, and has his head propped up with a hand while he studies me. Normally I might find this creepy, but lately I've been doing a similar thing while he sleeps. I flush as happiness ripples over me. It's surreal that the day has finally arrived.

Mason and I have been together for six years and engaged for the last two. He dragged his feet so long to set a date for the wedding, my mother was positive we were heading for a breakup. She wasn't far off base. I didn't tell anyone, but we hit a rough patch a year ago and broke up for two weeks. He wasn't sure he believed in the institution of marriage, and I told him if he wanted to be with me, he better start believing in it fast. My ultimatum led to the breakup, but two weeks apart was more than enough time for us to realize we were both being idiots.

When we finally talked after our separation, I told him I realized that I didn't need a stupid piece of paper to prove we belong together. And he told me he realized that if it was just a dumb piece of paper, he'd rather get married than be without me.

I sleepily murmur, "Good morning," and he leans forward to brush his lips against mine.

My body hums alive, and I wish we had time for a morning romp. I peek over his shoulder at the alarm clock—shit, nope. My alarm is going off in minutes.

"Good morning, babydoll. You ready for today?" It's a serious question, but the twinkle in his eyes shows me he knows I'm ready. I've been ecstatic for days now.

Yawning into a smile, I can't resist teasing him. "Maybe. It depends on what you got me as a wedding gift."

His devilish grin in response might have concerned me any other day, but he can't cause too much trouble since most of today is scheduled down to the minute. Our wedding planner is very precise.

He kisses me on the nose. "I have two gifts today."

Uh oh. I only got him one. I'm cautious with my "Two?" They better be small. I got him the expensive telescope he's been drooling over. It's a marvelous gift, but hopefully he didn't go overboard.

He nudges me onto my back and kisses me deeply for a few moments, and a punch of desire burns in my core. I moan as he nibbles his way down my neck. "Your first gift is that today is a freeuse day."

My pussy clenches with need. Ohhh, what's this? Ever since the short breakup, we've been trying to spice things up in the bedroom. We've experimented with freeuse, where he spends a day using me however he wants. I revel in it. We've also been talking about me being a hotwife... after we're married. I joked that we had to wait because I wasn't a wife yet, but I'm sure we'll try that soon. I have a kink about feeling like a sex toy and just a hole to be used, so freeuse days are always fun. It's not something I want all the time, but occasionally it's thrilling and naughty to be objectified.

Excitement swirls in my core when he slips a hand under my nightshirt and plays with my nipples. If he intended to get me horny this morning, he succeeded. I'm groggy and the haze of lust makes it difficult to think, but we can't do freeuse right now.

"Mason..."

He sucks lightly on my neck as shivers run down my spine. "Yes, Vanessa?"

Fuck, he better not give me a hickey. I shove on his head. "We have a schedule. We can't do freeuse today."

He stops sucking and peers up at me. "Sure we can. I promise not to mess up the schedule. Does that work?"

My wet pussy says it works very well. Fuck it. I laugh at him. "Okay, I'm yours for our wedding day then."

"You're mine every day," he announces as he swoops down to kiss and lick my neck again.

The loud beeping of my alarm clock makes me giggle as I shut it off. "Okay, enough of that. It's time to get up!"

It might be mean of me, but his groan gives me great satisfaction as we both get out of bed for the big day.

The ceremony is perfect, despite the inevitable tiny mishap that always seems to happen. Stephanie, a bridesmaid, forgot her shoes at home and had to beg her cousin to switch shoes with her so she didn't wear flip-flops during the ceremony.

The hotel is gorgeous, and the decorations are exactly what I selected. The devotion I feel for Mason as I walk down the aisle tells me I'm making the right choice. There's no hesitation on his part during our vows, and I can see adoration written all over his face.

Our reception will serve dinner and feature an open bar with live music. While the groomsmen usher the guests to the reception hall, Mason and I duck into a bathroom to freshen up. I plan to wear my wedding dress for part of the night and then change into something more comfortable.

The bathroom is fairly large, with four stalls and a vanity with a row of sinks below the mirror. I'm at the sink fixing my makeup and watching Mason take an "out of order" sign that is leaning against the wall, open the A-frame sign, and set it right in front of the door outside the bathroom. It's a little unnecessary since we won't be in here long, but whatever, that's Mason.

He's relaxed and happy as he moves behind me and kisses my neck. "Well, we're married."

Mmmm, I adore it when he nibbles and kisses right there. He always knows the perfect spot. Gentle waves of delight radiate through me from his touch.

I wash my hands and smile softly. "Yep."

Without warning, he shoves my shoulder to the counter, and I swallow my gasp. Oh shit, he's fucking me right now? My legs quiver and all gentleness leaves my body as passion takes over. This is dirty and hot.

He yanks up my white wedding dress and bunches the lace and tulle around my waist, and I squirm with need at the rough treatment. I'm wearing white, satin panties, and he rubs my pussy for a moment as a damp patch grows with each stroke. Shit, this is going to be something to remember from our wedding day. He wants me to ignore what he's doing, but it's tough to do that when my face is against the bathroom counter.

His voice is deceptively casual. "What was your favorite part of the ceremony?"

Pings of bliss shoot to my toes, and I try not to moan. Uh, how am I supposed to think while he's driving me wild with his fingers? I wrack my brain.

When he speeds up, I blurt out, "The vows."

I'm proud of myself for coming up with a quick answer.

He fumbles with opening his pants before pushing aside my panties. When the head of his cock fits against my wet slit, I almost lose it and moan from the joy.

"So, what was it about them that made it your favorite part?"

Damn him. He presses the tip inside me and all thoughts drain from my head from the delight.

He pulls out. "I'm waiting."

Ugh. Okay, I can do this. "I liked the—" He slams his cock inside me, and I can't hold in my cry of elation. "Ohhhhh, god."

He sets a frantic pace, as if he's in a competition of who can come the quickest, and the assault on my pussy has me breathless and dizzy.

"Vanessa... I'm still waiting."

I grip the edge of the counter and hold on as he plows into me relentlessly. How is he not winded? "I liked..." I almost lose my train of thought again from ecstasy as he slams into me. "... Liked your personalized vows."

Pings of bliss flutter from my core, and right when I get close to my orgasm, he groans out, "Oh fuck, babygirl, I'm coming!" and fills my pussy with his warm cum.

He slowly fucks me as he comes down from his orgasm and when he withdraws, he slaps my ass. "I'm done with you. Let's get back to the reception."

My entire body cries out in displeasure and I'm desperately horny. Holy shit, why did I agree to freeuse today? I'm so out of it, he has to help adjust my panties and straighten my dress. I'm flustered and dazed when I look in the mirror.

Mason must sense that I'm nervous about my appearance. He kisses my cheek and whispers, "You look beautiful, and having my cum dripping out of you is going to make you feel even sluttier than being used in the restroom."

Our combined juices leak out of me, and my nipples harden. Shit, he's right.

The reception is a blur of sexual excitement and laughter, and I wish Mason would take me upstairs and fuck me right now because I need to come so badly. I didn't think I would get edged on my wedding day. But, sadly, we have to stay long enough for dinner and to cut the cake. The catering company did an incredible job: the salmon is delicious, and the cake looks like it's right out of a magazine. Even so, all I can think about is fucking my new husband.

After they clear our plates, Mason leans over to me. "Do you want to know what your second gift is?"

Ooooh, it's gift time! The telescope is waiting at home, but I can tell him what it is, if he wants to know. "Sure, tell me."

He moves closer and his whisper tickles my ear. "Now that we're married, you're a hotwife."

I'm unsure what to say for a moment. What sort of gift is this? Like, ohhh sure, someday I'll fuck other guys and get my kicks, but it doesn't seem like much of a gift since we already discussed doing it after the wedding. At least my telescope is an actual gift.

It doesn't matter though, I love him even without a tangible gift. I smile indulgently at him. "Okay, I'll be your hotwife anytime you want. Do you want to know what yours is? It's at home."

"Well, don't you want to hear what the rest of your gift is?"

Oh, there's more. I give him a quick peck on the lips. "What's the rest?"

"See the table over there?"

He points to the table where all four groomsmen are sitting and laughing. His best friend, Aaron, catches my eye, and I swear his eyes smolder. My nipples harden, and I feel a blush creep up my face.

Okay, that's odd. "Yeah, I see the table with your friends."

"They are your wedding gift."

My pussy clenches from desire, but I'm confused. He can't mean what I think he does. "Uh... what?"

He kisses my ear, and his voice is husky. "In an hour, we're going to leave the party, and they're going to join us in our room to fuck you and turn you into a hotwife. I want your first time to be with people I trust."

My mind blanks for a moment, and I stare at him wide-eyed. I should probably thank Nadia for this.

A few weeks ago, on a bachelorette weekend in the mountains, one bridesmaid, Nadia, visited the neighboring cabin and, by her account, had a pretty thrilling time with ten men. When I got home, it was all I could think about. I dreamed about fucking multiple men, and when Mason and I made love, I imagined other guys in the room. I eventually told Mason about my slutty fantasy, and he asked if I'd do it if he arranged it. In a moment of horniness, I said yes, but only after we were married. I didn't expect it to happen on our wedding night.

Mason reaches for my hand in my lap and squeezes it. "Do you want to fuck four men as your gift?"

Every fiber of my being screams with delight, but only a whisper comes out.

"Yes."

Chapter 2

Before we leave the reception, I gather my bridesmaids together to thank them and dish about my wedding present. Nadia gives me a high five, but everyone else is shocked. I'm glad at least one friend supports my kinky plans.

When I rejoin Mason, once we decide it's acceptable for us to duck out of the reception, we sneak upstairs. In the elevator, he gives me the option of having tonight recorded on video, and there is zero hesitation with my yes. Proof of me fucking four guys that I can rewatch in the future? Hell, yes.

In the room, he tells me to take a nice, long, relaxing shower because Jose, a groomsman, is loaning us his video equipment for the night, and he's going to come help set it up. I'd rather not witness two men fiddling with electronics, so I'm happy to hide in the bathroom. I also want to gather my thoughts before the afterparty starts.

The shower refreshes me, and I'm practically vibrating with need as I put on the white lingerie set that I bought especially for tonight. It's a sheer negligée with a wisp of fabric that they called a G-string but is mainly a joke, along with the matching robe. I kept my blonde hair in a topknot in the shower, so it didn't get wet, but I know it's eventually going to fall down during the evening if I'm fucking four guys. I eye my hair critically in the mirror before unwinding it and putting it in a ponytail. This is so dirty, and Mason's bedroom shenanigans this morning kept me on a low simmer all day. Add in the actual edging in the bathroom before the reception, and I'm like a match ready to be lit on fire.

Spreading my fingers on my left hand, I admire the glint of my newly acquired wedding band. Thank God, I'm finally married. I wasn't sure it was ever going to happen, and it almost didn't. After our two-week breakup we did couples counseling, during which he admitted to hooking up with multiple women while we were apart. I'd spent the time with my face in a carton of cookie dough ice cream, sobbing, and binge-watching romantic comedies.

It took me a little while to accept that everyone processes hurt in their own way, but it still perturbed me when I found out he had a threesome with twins. We had never discussed bringing a third into the bedroom, though if we had, I would have wanted it to be another man. That led us to discussing me being a hotwife or having a threesome. Mason claims he gets super hot at the thought of me with other men, but I need to see it to believe it. I guess I'll find out tonight.

Smoothing the fabric of the robe down my thighs, I adjust the bow I made with my robe's belt to make sure it's perfect. It's been a long day, and I expected to be exhausted by now. Instead, I'm energized and looking forward to the wedding gift from my husband.

I fight the urge to reapply my makeup. There really is no point since I'm about to get thoroughly fucked. Butterflies dance in my stomach, and I'm trembling when I smile at myself in the mirror before leaving the bathroom. Am I insane for doing this?

The honeymoon suite is a wedding gift from his parents, and it's nicer than any room I've ever rented before. There is a separate master bedroom with two large, overstuffed chairs in a corner. The king-size bed dominates the room, and the mirrors on the wall opposite the bed are low enough that we can watch ourselves fucking. I giggled as soon as I saw the mirrors earlier. The room is exactly what I would want for my wedding night.

As I walk out of the bathroom, I see Mason over by the window with Jose, setting up a video recorder. An unexpected third person catches my eye and startles me. "Shit, Stephanie. I didn't see you there."

Stephanie, the bridesmaid who forgot her shoes, gives a frosty smile. "I helped Jose carry the equipment from his car."

I perch on the edge of the bed and feel a flash of annoyance. Something about Stephanie's expression irks me. Is she judging me? She's rigid and obviously uncomfortable as she shifts impatiently. I shouldn't have spilled the beans to all the bridesmaids about Mason's wedding present to me.

Stephanie scowls at Jose. "You almost done?"

Dang, what burr got up her ass? And where is her hunky husband? She's continually raving about her spectacular marriage and her sexy, wonderful husband who will do anything for her. Why is she up here with Jose and not with Mr. Perfect?

Jose's melodic tone entrances me. "We're about finished — be patient."

He could talk to me every day, and I'd never tire of hearing his voice. It hits a little differently tonight, knowing he's going to fuck me. My pussy gets wet as I imagine him whispering sweet nothings while he's plowing into me.

Jose startles me when he whoops out a "Done!" and I can sense Stephanie's sigh of relief.

Oh yeah, Little Miss Perfect Marriage is judging my harlot soul for wanting to fuck all the groomsmen, but I don't care. This is my life. If I wanted to get railed by an entire football team, it would still be none of her business.

Mason follows Jose and Stephanie towards the door. When he passes me, he bends over to kiss my neck and whispers, "I'll be right back with the men."

My pussy buzzes and my nipples harden while my brain freezes from how hot this is. Since I can't think, all I do is give him a brief nod as they leave me alone. The soft click of the hotel room door jolts me out of my stupor. Holy fuck, it's almost time.

CHAPTER 3

I have too much energy to sit still, so I jump up and pace in front of the bed. It's not long before I hear the door open and all the groomsmen come in, laughing at some joke. Jose and Mason are the last ones into the room, and the three in front all stop when they see me.

"Wow." Aaron whistles softly. "You're gorgeous."

A jolt of lust has me trembling. Since he's Mason's best friend, he sees me more often than the other guys. I was afraid this would be awkward, but the appreciation in his glance makes my pussy throb. I've always been curious about whether he was good in bed. He's an incredibly kind person, and I assume he's a giving bedmate and focuses on the woman's fulfillment. Tonight is my chance to find out.

Leo and David are twins, and I'm secretly pleased that I get to fuck twins. It only seems fair, since Mason did. Not that anyone is keeping score, but it feels like the universe is balancing our sexual exploits. Leo and David are identical, but they're easy to tell apart. David has an active job, so he's fit, while Leo has a desk job and has a soft dad bod. I don't know them that well, but I trust Mason to choose the right guys for me.

Mason weaves between the men and comes in close to kiss me passionately. His tongue plunders into my mouth, and I'm lightheaded. I sway towards him while he continues to ravage me. When he brings a hand up to my breast, cups it, and gives it a light squeeze, knowing the men are watching causes an illicit thrill to zip between my legs.

He breaks off the kiss and murmurs, "I'll be in the room the entire time. Okay?"

I nod breathlessly as he shrugs out of his tuxedo coat and sits in one of the oversized chairs. Neediness consumes me as he loosens his bowtie and uncuffs his sleeves so he can roll them up. He's methodical in his process, and I watch him while all the groomsmen stand there, drinking me in with thirsty eyes but not speaking. After Mason unbuttons his shirt and untucks it from his pants, he leans back, linking his hands and resting them on his stomach. What's going on?

He grins at me before addressing the men. "I want you all to undress her slowly. Give me a good show since I'm sharing my freeuse slut with you tonight."

My pussy clenches, and moisture leaks down my inner thigh at his words. Ohhhh fuck, he's taking part? When he sat down, I assumed he was going to watch and stay silent. He knows being called a slut drives me wild, but he's never done it in front of other people. His words ping a part of my brain, and I really do feel like a slut. One who wants the men to use any hole they desire to fill.

The men surround me, leaving room for Mason to see me clearly. Was this all pre-planned? My head spins as Jose plucks the bow of my robe open while the twins move behind me. One of them kisses my neck, and I tilt my head to the side to give him better access.

Four sets of hands roam my body, and I close my eyes and groan from the pleasure. Holy fuck, this is erotic. Since I can't see, I don't know who is doing what, and someone pushes my robe down. It falls to the floor, and moist lips press against my now-bare shoulder.

Since Jose was in front of me, I assume it's his hands that cup my breasts and tweak my nipples. Someone runs a hand down my front and inside my panties, and I spread my legs apart so he can slip his fingers between my wet folds. Bliss builds in my core, and I moan as a thumb caresses my clit softly.

"Kiss her," Mason demands, and my eyes fly open as Jose brushes his lips against mine.

I was right. It's Jose's hands on my breasts, and as he deepens the kiss, I melt towards him. Someone behind me pulls up my negligee, and multiple hands massage my ass. I sigh in ecstasy as the person rubbing my clit speeds up. The longer the kiss goes on with Jose, the wetter I get. I didn't think it was possible to get more turned on, but I'm desperate to be fucked and growing needier by the moment.

This is fucking amazing. I close my eyes again, letting the sensations surge over me. The twins are being thorough in their exploration, and when one of them slides a digit into my wet pussy from behind, I squeal into Jose's mouth. He breaks off the kiss with a laugh, and he helps someone remove my negligee over my head.

This time, when Mason gives direction, I don't open my eyes. "Remove her panties."

Fingers hook into both sides of the fabric and drag them down my legs. They're so tiny, I don't even bother stepping out of them.

"Isn't my wife lovely?"

The guys murmur agreements, but it's Aaron's "Yes, she is" directly in front of me that makes me open my eyes.

I hadn't noticed that Jose moved to the side, and Aaron's mesmerizing brown eyes bore into mine. My breath catches, and my body tingles. Aaron's dress shirt is open, and he removed his undershirt at some point. His dark-brown skin contrasts with the whiteness of the shirt, and I want to stroke his well-defined chest. I raise my hands and almost touch him, then drop them again. I'm not sure I'm allowed to do anything but stand here.

I sneak a look at Mason, intending to question him, and get another shock. Mason has his thick cock out, and he's stroking while staring straight at me. Oh fuck, that's hot.

He smiles at me. "Babydoll, did you want to touch him?"

Fuck yes, I do. I keep my voice neutral when I reply — in case he doesn't want me to be too enthusiastic. "May I please?"

His grin gets bigger. "Yes. Take his shirt off and kiss his chest."

I lock onto Aaron's gaze again as I nudge his shirt off his shoulders and tug it down his arms. I drop it on the floor with all of my clothes. The other guys are stripping, but I barely notice. I've only got eyes for Aaron as I run my hands up his chest. His skin is warm and soft, and his muscles jump as I lean in to plant a kiss next to one of his nipples. Mason can't see what I'm doing, and I dart my tongue out to give him a lick as well.

"Now remove his pants," Mason groans, and more wetness leaks down my thigh.

Does he enjoy watching me undress his best friend? As I unbuckle Aaron's belt and unzip his pants, the other guys caress me again. A quick look at them tells me that everyone is undressed except Aaron and Mason. I wish I could be in Mason's position and watch the men play with me, but I guess that's what the video is for. I'll be able to relive this and remember how it felt... and it's so fucking fabulous.

It's only six hands on my body, but it's complicated to keep track of them. One is between my legs and brushing my clit from the front, and another hand is coming at my pussy from the back and finger fucking me with two digits. Someone has both hands wrapped around me and is playing with my nipples. Longing builds in my core and I sway on my feet as the sensations threaten to overwhelm me. I have to shake my head to focus on my task of stripping Aaron.

As I sweep Aaron's pants down, I hook onto his boxers and take them off at the same time. His thick cock springs free, and he takes a step closer to me so that the tip grazes my belly. He's got a gorgeous, well-shaped shaft with a slight upward curve to it. If I didn't have all these hands fondling me, I would sink to my knees and beg to suck him.

Mason's voice cracks. "Do you like his cock, babydoll?"

Before I answer, I look at Mason. He's stroking his shaft slowly, with a lust-glazed hunger in his eyes. Oh yeah, he's loving this.

Beaming sweetly at him, I purr, "It's magnificent. May I rub it?"

"Yes," he breathes, and I don't wait for further instruction. Using both hands, I caress Aaron's length and gently cup his balls. Aaron's gulp of air tells me he wasn't expecting a thorough inspection, and he closes his eyes, clearly enjoying every stroke.

I'm momentarily distracted because one twin starts kissing any part of my body he can reach, and I tilt my head to give him access to my neck. All the men touching me drives me close to an orgasm. I rock my hips, forcing the fingers in my pussy to fuck me faster. I can't handle much more of this. He better let me have a cock inside of me soon.

Mason clears his throat. "So, my little freeuse slut. I have a surprise for you tonight."

What's this? I blink at Mason. Getting fucked by four guys isn't enough of a surprise?

He smiles wickedly. "I bet you didn't know that David enjoys tying his girlfriends up."

Oh, hell yes. I'm getting tied up along with all this? I stay calm as I reply, "No, I didn't."

My eyes widen as everyone stops what they're doing, and Aaron takes my hands and holds them together. This all seems choreographed, like Mason went over the evening with everyone. The groomsmen are all being careful to leave a clear line of sight for Mason and the video camera next to him. He's not telling them exactly what to do and they seem to know. They're not talking unless asked a question, so that must have been part of the discussion. It's like we're all Mason's puppets tonight, and it's erotic knowing this wasn't a last-minute gift he thought of this morning. Hmm, how long ago did he plan this?

When David shows up at my side with a cord and begins binding my wrists in front of me, I'm 100 percent positive this was all pre-planned. He makes quick work of tying my wrists up and tests that the binding isn't too tight. Now that David is visible, I inspect his cock to see what he's packing. No one would blame me for being curious.

He's an adequate size, with thick veins standing out that I wish I could skim my fingers over. But with my hands bound, I don't think I'm going to be touching anything. I squeeze my thighs together, thinking of him sliding inside me. Do identical twins have identical cocks? Now I'm curious to see Leo, but he's behind me so I have to wait until he moves.

Mason continues to stroke himself, and I keep peeking over at him. All these hands on me and knowing I'm going to be fucked by four men makes me want Mason even more. This is going to feel amazing, but I really need my new husband's cock inside me tonight as well. I'm hoping he plans to use me after the other men are done.

"Do you guys think my freeuse slut is ready to be fucked?"

I focus on Aaron when they all respond with various forms of agreement, and his eyes glow with desire. Did he want to fuck me before given this chance, or did he only want me after Mason made the offer? I'll probably never know, but he's a very willing participant. Shit, this better not make doing things with him awkward in the future. But even if it does, I don't think I would say no to tonight. I'm flushed and trembling with need for all these men.

"Babygirl, I want you to get on the bed on your back. David will secure your wrists to the headboard. Use your safeword if you need us to stop. Understand?"

I break off eye contact with Aaron and shine all my love towards Mason. "Yes, I understand."

Crawling on the bed to the center, I wiggle my ass and get a nice, sexual zing from knowing the guys are watching me. I'm almost blinded by my hunger, and everything is hazy. I'm beyond caring about anything except getting a cock inside me. The foreplay of them undressing me ramped me up to a ten on the neediness scale, and I might combust the moment someone fucks me.

As soon as I'm settled on the bed, David climbs up by my head and raises my wrists. He uses more cord to attach my already-bound-together wrists to the headboard. His cock wags close to my face, and I could probably shift and suck on it. Raising my head, I glance at Mason and he's watching me intently. I give my dear husband a huge grin, turn my head, and lick David's cock.

David jerks, and his sharp intake of breath almost makes me giggle. I peek to see Mason's response to my antics.

He's not stroking, and his eyes narrow. He studies me for a moment before commanding, "Suck on it."

Mmmm, yeah, he doesn't have to force me to do this. David moves a little closer, making it easier for me to engulf the tip. He's salty with pre-cum, and I swirl my tongue on the underside of his cock while he presses in further. He kneels next to me, so he can fuck my mouth with shallow thrusts while two pairs of hands tug my legs open. I'm too busy with David, so I don't pay attention to who is doing what at the end of the bed, but it's Aaron who climbs between my legs.

Bending my knees, I open myself as wide as I can while Aaron fits the head of his cock against my slick opening. I moan, "Ohhhh, god," around David's shaft as Aaron sinks into me. The pleasure is so intense my vision blurs and the room tilts. Aaron is thicker than Mason, so when Aaron props himself up on his arms and drills into my pussy, his cock stretches me out more than I've ever been before.

As Aaron speeds up, so does David. I thought I wanted all four guys to unload in my pussy, but the longer David fucks my mouth, the more I'm craving him to blow his load in my throat. It's not really about where they come, it's more about how dirty and slutty I'll feel from them using various holes. I'm not sure if the guys realize that tonight is all about me. Mason might be the director, but he's doing this for me. This is only happening because Nadia's experience in the cabin was such an enormous turn-on.

The guys might not be speaking, but as David and Aaron fuck me, they moan loudly, and hearing two men enjoying me at the same time spirals me closer to my orgasm. I didn't explode immediately when Aaron entered me, but I'm not going to last long. Aaron picks up speed, and it seems like he's going to come soon. I'm chanting "Fuck me," but since David's cock is in my throat all the way to the base, it's garbled nonsense.

When I try to move my legs to wrap around Aaron, two people grab my ankles and hold my feet down to the bed. Helplessness washes over me, and I arch my back as electricity shoots to my toes. Oh god. Being totally restrained with a guy fucking my mouth and another in my pussy is the right type of dirty. I close my eyes as my orgasm hits me, and I cry out around David's shaft as my entire body convulses from rapture.

David groans and his cock pulses against my tongue while spurts of his cum coat the back of my throat, and a few seconds later, Aaron shouts out his own "Oh god" as he unloads his cum deep into my pussy. He whacks against my sodden hole a few more times before pulling out, and I eagerly lick and suck on David, cleaning him off. I'm not hating David's cum, but Mason tastes better.

When David pulls out and gets off the bed, I lift my head to make sure Mason is okay with everything. He's still stroking his cock, but he's got the pained look on his face he always gets when he's trying not to come. Oh yeah, he's still doing fine.

The men let go of my ankles, and Jose mounts the bed. Instead of leaving my legs down, he presses them up towards my chest as he slides into my pussy. "Ohhh, fuck," I groan as he hammers into me. Jose is an enthusiastic lover. He's fucking me so hard and fast, I have to close my eyes to avoid becoming overwhelmed by everything. Each stroke shoots pleasure down to my toes, and I'm quickly ramping up to a second orgasm. I keep expecting Leo to come fuck my face after his brother did, but to my disappointment, he doesn't.

I flex my hips and meet Jose's thrusts, trying to force him as deep as he can go. I need him to hold on until I come again, and I'm begging "More, please" over and over. This might be the hottest thing I've done in my life. I can't think of any sexual experience that tops this.

Tension coils in my belly, and my breath runs ragged. A rush of joy causes stars to twinkle at the edge of my vision. The twins move to each side of me on the bed and suck on my nipples. The combined assault of their mouths and Jose's cock is more than I can take, and my second orgasm rips through me.

I squeal and moan in delight as I buck my hips, and my body trembles with the strength of my climax. Time holds no meaning as Jose continues to fuck me. His rhythm is punishing, and the sounds of him slapping into my wet pussy fill the room along with his groans. He comes with a roar, and Leo kisses me deeply as Jose spasms and fills me with his cum.

I open my eyes when he withdraws his cock, and the combined wetness from the two men slips out of me and runs down my crack. I want to squirm from how filthy it feels. Jesus Christ, I've had the cum of three men on my wedding night, none of which are my husband. This is so fucking slutty, and I love it.

The twins are still on the bed with me, and I look towards Leo, assuming it's his turn. He smiles and rolls me onto my side facing away from him. David tweaks and plays with my nipples and kisses me again. Our tongues twist together, and Leo lies behind me with his cock poking my ass. He better not be trying to fuck that hole without lube. Thankfully, when he readjusts, I can tell he's going for my pussy.

Raising my leg, Leo slides into me, and we both moan from the pleasure. This is one of my favorite cuddle-fuck positions, and I curl my leg behind his to keep my thighs spread. He grabs my hip and drills into me while David sucks on my nipple again.

I'm chanting "Oh, fuck" while the smack of my skin against Leo mingles with his moans. I try to see how Mason is taking this, but David is in my way, so I close my eyes and enjoy the men using me. David holds onto my breast, so it doesn't jiggle with Leo's vigorous thrusts, and the perfect amount of suction from his mouth sends tingles straight to my pussy, where his brother is bucking against me wildly. Right when I'm on the brink of another orgasm, Leo groans, and his sticky seed coats my cave walls.

Ugh, fuck. I was soooo close to coming. I mewl out in distress when he pulls out. This better not be over. I need to come again.

David presses my shoulder. I roll onto my back, and he moves his mouth to my other nipple as Aaron gets on the bed between my legs again. Uhh, what the fuck? The men get seconds?

Mason must have sensed my confusion. "That's right, use my slut all you want, guys. She's yours for the taking tonight."

Ohhhh, fuck. I don't know why I assumed each guy only got one go at me. I close my eyes as Aaron slides into me again. He's fully erect, and knowing he's fucking two other guys' cum back into me is so filthy, I explode around his cock, and my brain switches off.

Ecstasy bursts through me, and everything becomes a blur as the guys continue to use me. At one point, I suck on Leo's cock while his brother fucks me. Their cocks are similar enough that if they were at the same fitness level, I don't think I would have been able to tell the difference between them in the dark.

I don't know how long everything goes on, but it seems like they use me for hours. I lose track of my orgasms after the fifth one, and by the end, it's waves of unending rapture. When they stop, I barely notice. Someone unties me and the room gets quiet. I settle onto my stomach and fall asleep, totally spent.

I'm woken up as Mason slides his cock into me. He covers my body with his and uses his body weight to press me down into the bed. My pussy is tender from the continual poundings, but his gentle prods as he stretches me only give me pleasure. He and I have an agreement that he can fuck me in my sleep during freeuse days, so I'm not surprised that he's doing just that. It hits a pretty big kink of mine, and I moan softly and murmur his name as he slowly fucks me.

"Vanessa, you know I love you so much. Don't you?"

Between moans, I murmur, "Yes, Mason."

Layers of pressure build in my core, and every part of me buzzes with bliss. He could fuck me all night long if he wanted, and I wouldn't complain. He rocks against me, and each nudge deep inside me pushes me towards a gentle climax. I peak again right before he comes, and I cry out as I quiver from the intense orgasm.

He groans when he knows I've come, and his cock pulses as he fills me with his cum. He relaxes over me, and his shaft spasms, releasing every drop inside my pussy. When he finally slips out, he kisses my neck and rolls to his side, taking me with him until we're spooning.

I'm immediately half asleep again, but he jostles me a little to wake me up.

"Vanessa... babygirl, are you okay?"

I smile dreamily, even though he can't see it. "Mmm, yes. Best present ever."

He chuckles and snuggles me tighter. "Well, don't get any bright ideas of doing this again. I'm not sure I want to share you with more than one guy at a time."

His statement wakes me, and I almost giggle. Who does he think he's fooling? The pure lust I saw on his face while the guys were pawing me told me he was all in for what was going on.

I take his hand and kiss his palm. "I know. It was a one-time deal."

"Yeah," he says gruffly. "You're mine."

I nibble on one of his fingers playfully before responding. "Yes... yours." I don't add that he's mine now as well. That's what being married to me means.

He kisses my neck, and I hum with approval. He and I both know there is no way in hell this won't happen again. But next time, I'm going to make him ask for it. This new hotwife knows how to play the long game.

As he relaxes fully, and I melt back into him, I think about the video of tonight and how much fun it's going to be to watch over and over again.

Oh yeah, best wedding gift ever.

The End

PLEASING THE CROWD

CHAPTER 1

My phone beeps that I have a text message, but I ignore it. Who in the fuck is texting me at 8 a.m. on a Saturday? No one I need to talk to, that's for damn sure. My husband, Cameron, and I had to get up early today because we have our second wedding of the weekend to attend. After the shitty week I've had, attending yet another frivolous, waste-of-money event isn't high on my to-do list.

I was a bridesmaid yesterday for my friend, Vanessa. Her sugar daddy's parents are so rich, they had a live band and an open bar with unlimited drinks. The amount of booze downed last night could have easily paid our rent for three months. Thank God I'm not a bridesmaid tonight — I wouldn't have been able to afford another dress.

I lean on the counter and stare in the mirror. Luckily, I don't look as tired as I feel. Earlier this morning, I pulled my long brown hair into a high ponytail and put on stretch pants and a tank top, intending to do a little housecleaning after breakfast. A fight with Cameron changed my plans, and I've been hiding in the bathroom for 30 minutes to avoid him. We've been bickering all week, and I don't want to admit what the real problem is.

I'm so fucking jealous of my friends getting married. It's not even funny.

My stomach tightens, and I grip the edge of the counter, wishing it was Monday already so I could put this shitty weekend behind me. I don't want to keep fighting, but how do I explain to my loving husband that I'm resentful that we didn't have a big wedding when it was my idea to elope at the courthouse?

Cameron and I have been together for five years, and he proposed two years ago. We planned to save up for a wedding since neither of our parents could help financially, but after a year went by and we still had very little put aside, I knew if I wanted to be his wife in this century, I had to give up my dreams of anything more than a potluck reception in my aunt's backyard.

We eloped, and a week later we had a reception for anyone who was willing to bring food and their own beer. I would've loved to have the huge wedding, bridesmaids, and a bachelorette weekend where everything was all about me. Our potluck reception at my aunt's house was a year ago, and now it seems like all my friends are getting married. Each joyful event I attend makes my lack of a wedding sting even more.

And I was a bitch to Vanessa last night, which doesn't help my mood this morning. She's the friend who had the amazing bachelorette weekend that was all about her. It was in a mountain cabin, and one of the other bridesmaids, Nadia, ended up fucking like ten guys in the cabin next to us, or some crazy shit like that.

I didn't even know Nadia had an open marriage, and it blew my mind when I found out. The way she described it was crazy hot, and it's all I've thought about since the trip. I love Cameron, but I'd like ten guys using me for a night and giving me more orgasms than I can count. Cameron would never go for it, so I can't even bring it up. Once your wife says she wants to fuck ten guys, where do you go from there? We'd probably end up divorced.

To top it all off, not only did Vanessa have the wedding of my dreams, but halfway through the reception, she gossiped to all us bridesmaids that her husband was 'gifting' her to all the groomsmen after the ceremony. I mutter to myself as jealousy burns in my stomach. Like, Jesus Christ... I can't even make this shit up.

After Vanessa told us the plans with the groomsmen, I kept checking them out and imagining it was me. Cameron got tipsy and horny, so he kept taunting me and saying he was going to use me and edge me when we got home. I planned to imagine a fantasy of me with all the groomsmen while Cameron did whatever he wanted to my eager pussy. He ruined it all by drinking too much and getting sick. A friend took him home while I stayed and finished my bridesmaid duties. I saw Vanessa right before she got to fuck all the groomsmen, and she looked stunning in a white lingerie set. Her husband even set up a video camera so they could watch it later. Why can't that be my life?

When my phone beeps again, I glance at the screen.

Ugh, it's Cameron.

I hop up on the counter and plant my ass without checking the message. I might just camp out in the bathroom all morning. Fuck him. At least our apartment has two bathrooms. He can use the other one until I feel like vacating this one. My phone has enough battery life, I could stay here for hours.

A knock on the bathroom door makes me jump.

"Stephanie, can we talk?"

I snort in reply. Guess he decided to stop texting me from across the apartment. We're only fighting because I'm in a bad mood. He just mentioned that he wouldn't drink tonight, and I got snotty after thinking about last night again. He snapped back at me, and now, here I am... hiding in the bathroom.

I sigh loudly. Shit, I'm not being fair. I married a wonderful man, and it's not his fault we both come from poor families. Even if we had saved up thousands for a wedding, we would have been smarter to put it down on a house or something else instead of blowing it on a big party. These are the same arguments I've been telling myself for months, but it still doesn't help the jealousy that consumes me at every wedding I attend.

Cameron knocks again. "Stephanie... baby, please, can we work this out? I'm sorry I got sick last night. I wanted to dance with you all night long. You looked so lovely."

Fuuuck, he thinks I'm mad because he got sick? He sounds so adorable and pathetic. I can already feel my anger draining away as I slide off the counter and open the bathroom door.

Cameron is standing there holding a bouquet of pink carnations that he obviously just bought at the grocery store around the corner. He got the cheap flowers because he knew I'd get even more pissy if he wasted money on expensive ones that wouldn't last as long. And pink is my favorite color.

My heart melts as I stare into his pleading puppy-dog eyes. Yeah, I can't stay mad at him.

"Oh Cam, I'm not angry because you got sick. I would have liked to dance with you, but it was free booze. Everyone was drinking too much."

He looks taken aback. "Then why are we fighting?"

I take the flowers from him and move past him to hide the flush of shame I can feel creeping up my cheeks. After setting the flowers on the counter, I dig a vase out from under the sink and fill it up with water.

I keep my tone neutral, not wanting to risk starting another fight. "It's been a long week. I told you work was stressful."

Work was actually less hectic than normal, but I don't want to admit to him the real reason I was so grumpy. I keep my back to him as I adjust the flowers in the vase, and he slides up behind me to kiss the back of my neck. I hold in a moan, close my eyes, and continue to arrange the flowers.

I may not fuck other men, but that doesn't mean our sex life is vanilla. Cameron heard that Vanessa and her new husband have freeuse days, and he and I have been trying that. From Friday to Sunday night was supposed to be freeuse for him, but his drinking messed up those plans.

As he presses his hardness against my ass, I imagine five guys in the doorway, watching. One thing that's funny about our relationship is that we both can go from annoyed to fucking in the blink of an eye. It makes for some fantastic angry sex, but almost all of my grouchiness faded once I saw the flowers. He's obviously not letting our tiff this morning stop anything.

Cameron nibbles on my neck. "Did you hear what Mason's wedding present to Vanessa was last night?"

I fight the urge to tip my head to give him better access and murmur, "Uh-huh, she fucked all the groomsmen."

He presses my shoulder towards the counter. I give zero resistance and lower my chest while my pussy tingles. Oh yeah, we're about to get fucked.

He grinds his cock into my ass. "Isn't that insane?"

"Yes... insane," I pant as pleasure swirls in my belly.

Fuck it, I can't pretend to ignore him anymore. I put my palms on the counter to gain leverage and thrust back as hard as I can.

When Cameron drags my stretch pants and panties down to my knees, I moan loudly. He's not usually this straight to the point with no foreplay unless we're having hot, quick, angry sex.

He backs off, and I watch him over my shoulder as he undoes his jeans. As he shoves them down, I take a step back and bend over fully, using the counter to support my head and forearms. Since my pants are only down as far as my knees, I can't spread my legs very wide, but Cameron doesn't care. He slides a finger into my pussy, and I gasp at the sudden contact. I'm so wet already, and I almost tell him I don't need warming up and to shove it in me, but I stop myself. Why would I tell him to stop pleasuring me? That's crazy talk.

Cameron spreads moisture from my pussy to my clit, and I moan as he brushes circles around my swollen bean.

His voice is husky. "I didn't know Vanessa was such a slut that she'd want to get fucked by a bunch of guys at the same time."

I can't tell if his tone is admiration for Vanessa or slut shaming, so I keep my opinion to myself. Yeah, it's slutty... amazingly slutty. I would have traded places with her in a heartbeat. Some of those groomsmen were smoking hot.

He moves his hand back to my pussy and finger fucks me roughly. "Do you think it's slutty that she had all those guys fucking her last night?"

My head reels, and it's difficult to determine how to respond. He's pleasuring me and talking about multiple men and one woman. How do I take this? When he adds in two more fingers, the thickness drives me wild, and I groan with longing.

Shit, let's just see what he says. "Yeah, Cam, a woman taking so many men at once is nothing but a little slut."

He removes his fingers and replaces them with his cock, slamming into me and shoving me against the counter. "Yeah, a slut who wants to be used."

He grasps my hips and hammers into me, and I hold on to the lip of the sink. I'm not wearing a bra under my tank top, and my breasts swing wildly with each vigorous thrust.

When he hits a sensitive spot, I gasp out, "A filthy whore who wants all her holes stuffed at once."

We haven't tried anal yet, but he loves it when I mention it in our dirty talk.

"Yeah," he huffs as he plows into me. "Such a filthy whore."

I can tell neither of us is talking about Vanessa anymore — not that I ever was. It was always me getting pounded by all the guys in my head, but I'm not sure who he's thinking about. Is it me, or is it a vague, generic, slutty woman?

Spikes of bliss travel through me, and I'm creeping towards my orgasm. I'm not sure if I prefer the fantasy of multiple men doing me at once, or if I prefer the idea of them in the doorway watching. Either way, this is a fantastic visual in my head, and it's helping me climax faster.

Cameron speeds up. "Tell me something, Stephanie...." I moan in response, and he continues. "Would you let me watch a guy fuck your pussy while you sucked on another guy's cock?"

Ohhh, god, would I. I'm not sure how enthusiastic I should sound, but when he smacks my ass, I squeal out a loud "Yes!" from the shock.

He keeps drilling into me. "Would you let my basketball buddies all take turns with you?"

The room tilts and my brain freezes. I forget how many friends he plays basketball with, but it's at least five guys.

He spanks me again, hard. The pain lights up my pussy, and I almost come. I groan, "Ohhh, fuck!"

"Would you, baby? Would you want to fuck all my friends?"

I'm close to coming, so I slip a hand down to caress my clit while he slams home several times, on the brink of his own orgasm.

"Tell me, Steph. Would you?"

His long groan makes one thing crystal clear. He's imagining me fucking all his friends, and the idea of it is about to make him come.

Knowing this is his fantasy, my orgasm jolts through me, and I cry out in a stream of words. "God, yes. I'd be your filthy whore and fuck all your friends all night long. Let them use whatever hole they want."

Euphoria surges over me while Cameron groans, "Such a dirty slut," as he explodes and paints my cave walls with his warm cum.

He fucks me for a few more thrusts as my pussy quivers around him, and my body shudders from the aftershocks of bliss. When he pulls out, he adjusts my panties and stretch pants back over my ass and holds onto me as he gently lowers us both to the floor. I sprawl half on top of him while we both try to catch our breath. As I rest my head on his chest, I can hear his heart rate slow down. Dang, I should get him to fantasize about me fucking other men more often.

We're both quiet for a bit, and he finally speaks. "Would you ever want to really do that?"

I debate for half a second before answering truthfully. "Yes, I would."

"How about tonight?"

What the fuck? His tone of voice is dry, so I can't tell if he's for real. I lean up on my arms and check his expression.

He's not joking.

Oh, hell yeah, I'm taking this chance before he changes his mind. I'm about to blurt out 'Yes' but change my tactic.

I keep my voice flirty. "Hmm, I don't know. Can they all wear suits so I can pretend I'm a bride?"

He snorts in amusement. "Yes, I could arrange that. We could do it after the reception tonight. Your own groomsmen."

Ohhhh, fuck yes!

I lay my head back on his chest and smile. "Okay, Daddy. Make it so."

He chuckles when he hears me say Daddy. I only use it when I really, really want something.

CHAPTER 2

I'm a wet mess the rest of the morning and afternoon. Cameron claims he has a lot of planning to do, and whenever I see him, he's hunched over his phone, his fingers racing like he's taking a typing test. If I wasn't so turned on, I'd be annoyed that he was ignoring me.

Do his friends even want to fuck me? Wait, are they even all single? Not that it's any of my business. I'm not the relationship police, and non-monogamy is becoming more popular in our age bracket.

I've never been invited to his basketball games, but that was okay—I like the fact that he has interests of his own that he doesn't need me for. I've always assumed his basketball buddies were casual friends he didn't see outside of the games, but apparently he's close enough to them that he seems to think they'll fuck me on short notice. If he dangles this carrot in front of me and doesn't deliver some men in suits, me and my pussy are going to be extremely disappointed.

I'm bursting to discuss this marvelous, new, slutty life with my best friend, Jasmine, and I wander into my bedroom for some privacy to call her. She was a bridesmaid for Vanessa too, and I'll see her at tonight's wedding since we run in one big circle of friends, but I need to talk to her now. I flop on the bed and clutch my phone to my ear.

Jasmine picks up after a couple of rings, and I can tell she's chewing gum from the snap of a bubble when she answers. "Yo, bitch. What's up?"

I fucking adore Jasmine. Half the time she looks and talks like she's the biggest bimbo on the planet. In reality, she's brilliant and working on her doctorate degree in psychology. She once told me she gets her kicks from men thinking she's a bimbo, and that's how she hooked up with her husband, Sebastian. He thought he was getting lucky and having a one-night stand with a hot, blonde airhead, but she ended up wrapping him around her little finger before he knew what hit him. He's a decent guy and is utterly devoted to her, so more power to them.

When she pops her gum in my ear again, I smile. "Jas, you're never going to believe the morning I had."

"Oh yeah? Tell me yours, and I'll tell you mine."

I explain the fight and everything leading up to Cameron fucking me senseless and me agreeing to sleep with his basketball buddies. The longer I talk, the more I think I sound crazy, and my stomach knots.

When I'm done explaining everything, Jasmine's screech of "No fucking way!" is so loud, I have to tear the phone from my ear.

I smile at her antics. Her reactions never disappoint me. "I'm serious. He's organizing it right now."

She's quiet for a minute. "Why do you think all our friends are experimenting with freeuse and group sex? Is a couple more likely to try it if their friends are doing it?"

Uh oh, she's focusing on the wrong thing. "Hey, Jasmine, listen for a second."

"Hmmm?" She still sounds distracted.

The knot in my stomach hardens. "Do you think I'm crazy to do this? Should I be asking you to talk me off the ledge? You're smart. Level with me here."

Her musical laugh relaxes me. "Steph, I can't say what's right for you. If at any point you don't want to do it anymore, call it off. But Nadia is living her best life fucking whoever she wants, so why can't we?"

My pussy buzzes at the thought of Nadia at the ski lodge with the 10 guys in the cabin. Yeah, it's still hot and I want to do it. Wait, is Jasmine thinking of fucking other guys as well? She said "Why can't 'we'."

"Jas, are you and Sebastian opening your marriage?" She giggles again, and the merry tinkle makes me smile; it's so damn contagious.

She gushes, "Oh no, but we're trying freeuse. Someone filled Sebastian's head with glorious stories at the wedding last night. He's already fucked me once today, and he's at the gym right now. He's always horny after he works out, so I'm expecting another pounding when he gets home."

She gives me graphic details about what happened to her in the kitchen this morning, and I'm oddly turned on. Should I be horny while thinking of my best friend fucking her husband? I want to rub my pussy through my panties, but no way in hell am I going to masturbate at the thought of Jasmine spread out on a table.

My clit throbs, and I swallow the excessive saliva in my mouth. What the hell is happening to me? I'm a sex-crazed version of myself. Fuck, I better get multiple cocks inside me tonight. I'm going to go insane with lust if I don't find an outlet soon.

Jasmine interrupts my thoughts. "Ohhh, I gotta go. I just heard the garage door. Love you!"

I barely have time to say goodbye before she disconnects. Heh, fine. Goodbye to you too. I roll onto my side, set the phone on the bed, and trace the outline of a rose on our floral comforter. I get lost in a daydream of being bent over the kitchen table while a parade of guys use me from behind. This isn't just a slutty thought. Deep down, I really am a slut.

Cameron strolls into the bedroom. "Hey, baby?"

I glance up at him in a sexual daze without responding. He stops and his eyes narrow while he studies me.

His face relaxes into a smile. "Someone appears to be all turned on. Were you thinking about all my friends fucking you?"

"Yes," I gasp out as he climbs into the bed behind me and rolls me onto my stomach. There is no foreplay. He yanks my pants and panties down just far enough to get access to my pussy. I'm so wet his cock slides right in, and we both moan as he sinks inside me. A zip of intense pleasure ripples from my pussy when he bottoms out.

His weight presses me down into the bed as he slowly fucks me, never pulling out all the way. The room spins with each nudge against my pussy. Shit, what if he doesn't let me come? Our freeuse weekend agreement was that he could fuck me all he wanted and not even let me come. Since I already had an orgasm this morning, it seems more likely he'd stop as soon as he blows his load into me right now.

Cameron places a firm hand on my shoulder and speeds up. "God, your tight pussy is so fucking wet."

I whimper as he uses me. Waves of delight build as he whacks against my pussy.

He fucks me in a quick, desperate rhythm that has me clawing at the comforter. "You were so fucking eager for my cock. This is what you want, isn't it?"

When I don't respond, he demands, "Isn't it?"

"Yes," I moan. "Fuck yes."

My climax is within reach, and his words are driving me closer to the abyss. When he slows down again, I can tell he's about to come.

He growls, "I married a filthy slut who wants to be used."

"Yes," I mewl out as I try to bump back against him in a desperate attempt to orgasm. If he'd hold on for a few more minutes, I could come.

"Steph, you'll do anything for this cock, won't you?"

Oh fuck, he's really getting into the dirty talk today. This is fabulous. "Yes... anything. God, please, can I come?"

He laughs harshly at my response and continues to drill into me slowly. "You'll even let me fuck your tight little ass if I want to. Admit it."

Ohhhh, shit. The pulse of rapture from my pussy almost overwhelms me, and I'm rushing towards my orgasm. I cry out, "Yes, anything. Please let me come."

With one final plunge, he roars and floods my pussy with its second load of cum today. Oh, holy fuck. I'm not going to come. Biting the comforter, I try to hide my moan of distress.

My entire body is lit up and every nerve ending pings as he stretches out next to me. My brain is mush, and I fight back tears. I was so damn close to coming; this is horrible. Whose idea was it to let him use me all he wanted this weekend?

I'm tense, and my body shudders from the stolen orgasm. A maelstrom of discontent swirls in my brain, and I take a moment to realize he's rubbing my back.

"Relax, baby. It will be okay. I promise."

He continues to snuggle me and murmur sweet nothings while I come down from my frenzy.

Eventually I take a deep breath and tease him. "If there haven't been multiple cocks in me by the end of the night, I'm going to be crabby."

He kisses the back of my head. "Oh, it's all arranged. You're going to have more cocks than you know what to do with."

Hmmm... we'll see about that. I don't voice the thought and snuggle closer to him, enjoying his warmth.

Chapter 3

Before we leave for the wedding, Cameron tells me that his friends will be at our house when we get back. He doesn't say how many he invited, and I don't ask since I want the surprise. God, I hope it's more than two. I want so many cocks there's a flood of cum all over me tonight. I don't know if this will ever happen again, so it needs to be good enough to satisfy me for years.

I'm sure the wedding is amazing, but my mind is a million miles away through the entire ceremony. Cameron holds my hand and occasionally gives me the side-eye, grins, and squeezes my fingers. We cut out from the reception as soon as the party is in full swing.

Jasmine catches me as we're leaving, and she hugs me with a hurried, "Goodbye and have fun!"

She's flushed and trembling, but before I can ask her what is going on, she whispers she'll see me tomorrow and runs off. Huh, something is definitely going on with her. I'll have to call her tomorrow.

My body is buzzing in the car, and I swear the drive home takes twice as long as it should. The house is quiet as we let ourselves in. Where are the guys?

I kick my high heels off. I'm about to question Cameron, but he speaks first. "The guys are in the den. Go get ready, and text me when you're done. I want to go talk to them."

He takes a few steps down the hall towards the den before turning back to me. He tips my chin up and kisses me deeply while my bare toes curl into the carpet.

"Steph, have fun tonight. I want to watch you come multiple times."

My nipples harden at his words, and I want to rub my thighs together. I give him a saucy "Yes, Daddy," and he laughs as heads to the den.

Once he's out of sight, I rush upstairs to the master bathroom, turn the shower on, and speed strip. I want a quick rinse before the men dirty me up again. I toss my hair in a bun so it doesn't get wet, and within a few minutes, I'm in the bedroom drying off.

I know exactly what I'm going to wear tonight. If I want to pretend to be a bride, I'm going to use the white lingerie I wore after our wedding a year ago. Even though we weren't having the big ceremony, I still wanted something special. I splurged on the most gorgeous, sheer teddy I could find. I haven't worn it since, which makes tonight seem like it really is my wedding night.

There isn't much to the outfit; it has molded lace cups with a front hook that brings the sides of the sheer fabric panel together. Someone could easily part the fabric and run their hands along my stomach. It ends at my hips, and there are matching g-string panties. I decide to skip them since I don't want to risk one of the men ripping the panties in their haste. If anyone is going to tear them off me, I want it to be Cameron.

I pace the room as my stomach flutters. Everyone is downstairs, waiting for my text, but I want to savor the anticipation for a few more minutes. Eyeing the bedroom critically, I decide the lamps should be on. I dawdle while making the room perfect by removing the throw pillows from the bed and turning the lamps on before dimming the overhead light. I'm not sure how to prepare my room for multiple men to fuck me.

Wait, maybe we should have done this in the spare room. Will I ever be able to make love with Cameron again without thinking about the other guys who fucked me in our bed? My pussy clenches, and a shiver runs down my spine. Hell, maybe that would be a good thing. It would add a little zing to our nights. Shit, I'm overthinking everything.

Sitting on the end of the bed, I admire myself in the full-length mirror on the opposite wall as I test out various poses for how I want to sit when all the men walk into the room. I'm looking and feeling sexy tonight, and I cross my legs and lean on one arm while I text Cameron.

I'm ready.

He doesn't respond to my message, but within a minute I hear the guys laughing and joking as they head upstairs towards the master bedroom. A thrill runs through me, and I catch my breath. That's more than just a couple of guys making that much noise.

Cameron leads the way, and five men in suits file in behind him. They stand behind Cameron, all facing me. Two of them look nervous and shift their weight from foot to foot.

I take the time to smile at each one of them and say, "Hi guys. Thanks for coming."

A naughty thrill zings through me. Holy fuck, I'm going to have six cocks in me tonight. I don't know anyone's names, but does it matter? The idea of five anonymous cocks inside me is dirty and awesome.

We all stare at each other in silence, and my heart races while wetness leaks from my pussy. Heh, panties might have been a good idea after all. Am I supposed to start the party?

Cameron clears his throat. "Stephanie, you have a choice tonight."

Ohhh, I get to decide something?

"Do you want to be blindfolded?"

Oh, fuck yeah! I'm about to blurt out my "Yes," but I hesitate and reconsider. If I'm blindfolded, I won't be able to see his enjoyment. I blink at him while my mind races. But it would be easier to imagine a slutty wedding fantasy where I'm a bride getting railed by all these men if I'm blindfolded.

Hell, let's do it. I grin. "Yes, please."

His eyes crinkle up at me. "Okay, I want you to lie in the middle of the bed."

Uncrossing my legs slowly, I stand up before crawling onto the bed. I feel six pairs of eyes following my every movement, and I'm breathless with need. Knowing they'll all have their hands on me soon is erotic as all fuck. I snake my way to the center and stretch out flat on my back, resting my hands on my stomach.

Cameron comes to the head of the bed and sits on the edge next to me. He pulls a long silky blindfold from his pocket before leaning over and kissing me softly.

"I love you, Steph."

Contentment washes over me at his words and I know he's going to do whatever he can to make tonight wonderful for me. I murmur, "I love you too," as he covers my eyes. I tilt up my head so he can wrap it around the back and secure it. He doubled up the fabric, and with the dim lights, I can't see anything. I wave a hand in front of my face to double check. Nope, not a thing.

The sound of rustling clothes fills the room, and Cameron leans over me and unhooks the front of my lingerie. He pushes the fabric to the side and exposes my breasts to the cool air and the men's vision. Since I'm not wearing panties, I'm essentially naked.

Cameron takes control. "Steph, spread your legs. Let the guys get a good look at you."

Shit, that's hot. I'm so turned on, they're going to get quite an eyeful. I spread my legs, and even though I can't see anybody, knowing they're all probably looking at my pussy causes an odd mixed feeling of vulnerability and eroticism. The mattress dips at my feet, like someone got on the bed. Oh, I guess we're starting.

Cameron leans close to my ear and whispers to me, "I want you to imagine that we just got married in the most beautiful ceremony. You were the gorgeous, blushing bride of your dreams."

Oh, fuck yeah, I can get into this fantasy. As he talks, I picture everything he's saying.

He continues. "The reception was perfect, and everyone had a great time. You and I snuck off early so we weren't exhausted."

Someone crawls between my legs and nudges them open even further so he can kneel between them. The tip of a cock runs up and down my wet slit, and I tremble from desire, imagining Cameron is about to fuck me for the first time as a married couple.

Cameron whispers more. "I blindfolded you so you could experience the pleasure and shut your mind off. Can you do that for me, Steph?"

I silently nod as the guy between my legs sinks his cock into me. Every inch stretches my pussy walls as he fills me, and I groan from the bliss. He's a lot thicker than Cameron, so it's difficult to stay in the fantasy that this is my wedding night. This is not Cameron in my pussy. The guy pulls my legs up as he thrusts slow and deep.

The bed on the other side of me dips, and someone leans over me as a wet mouth attaches to my nipple.

"Ohhhh, god," I moan, and Cameron takes the nipple closest to him in his mouth, swirling his tongue around the sensitive peak.

The onslaught of ecstasy from two men at my breasts and a guy with a gigantic cock in my pussy almost short circuits my brain. I arch my back and grip the comforter in my hands as bliss ripples up and down my body.

Cameron stops sucking on my nipple and kisses his way up my neck and whispers in my ear some more. "You looked so innocent and sweet in your wedding dress. But you and I both know you're just a filthy little slut. Don't we?"

I wasn't expecting the switch from loving to dirty talk, and my body hums in response. I speak in a normal tone so the other men can hear me clearly. "Yes, I'm a filthy slut who wants to be used."

The guy in my pussy takes my announcement to heart and speeds up, while the guy sucking on my tit tugs on my nipple with his mouth while I groan.

Cameron chuckles and uses a normal tone of voice again. "Well, in that case, open your mouth wide. Brad is going to shove his cock down your throat, and you're going to show everyone how well you can suck while getting your pussy pounded."

My mouth falls open from shock, but Cameron takes that as obedience, and he nudges the side of my head. I turn my face away from him as the bed jostles and a guy kneels next to me. As I wrap my lips around his fat cockhead and suck, my brain really does switch off. I become the fucktoy I wanted to be tonight.

The guy's cock is salty with pre-cum, and I gurgle happily around his thickness as the guy in my pussy speeds up more. He's plowing into me, knocking me around on the bed. The guy in my mouth buries his cock to the hilt, and I relax my throat so I don't gag on him. He pulls out and I try to keep the suction up so he can't remove his cock. He rewards me by sliding it back down my throat.

Cameron plays with my nipple, and I move a hand up to try and stroke his cock through his pants. "Oh no you don't." He laughs and pushes my hand away from his crotch.

I try to pout, but with the thick cock in my mouth, it's impossible. The pleasure builds, and I'm getting close to my orgasm. The massive cock inside me jerks a few times and a warmth floods my pussy. Ohhh, he came! The guy fucks me for a moment longer, pumping everything he's got before he climbs off.

The guy's cum slides out of me, and Cameron reaches down between my legs and massages some of it into my clit. I moan "Oh my god" around the cock in my mouth as his fingers create pings of bliss in my core.

"You like that, my slut?" Cameron growls.

I mewl out a tiny "Yes" as best I can, while someone else climbs between my legs.

This next guy doesn't tease me or wait, and I cry out from the sudden invasion of his savage thrusts. He's not as thick as the last guy, but he's still a good size, and he hammers away at my pussy while the guy in my mouth speeds up his face fucking. The first spurt of his cum hits the back of my throat as he groans.

I lick and suck for all I'm worth, trying to get all the cum. The guy at my breasts stops sucking, and when the cock from my mouth pulls out, I can tell the guy who was at my breast is next in line to use my mouth.

The absolute filthiness of the situation tips me over the edge as another cock eases between my lips. I buck and scream with pleasure as he fills my throat with his shaft, and the guy between my legs enthusiastically fucks me as the orgasm ripples through me from my fingers to my toes. It's a strong one, and the aftershocks continue while my mouth and pussy get used.

Cameron whispers in my ear again. "Just think, baby. I could roll you over and fuck your ass right now, and all you would do is beg me to use you harder. Wouldn't you?"

I try to nod and say yes, but the cock in my mouth prevents me. Cameron laughs, as if he can see my predicament.

His voice is thick with desire. "In fact, Steph, you're such a fucking whore you'd let us all fuck your ass and you'd beg for seconds."

While the two guys fuck me, I imagine all the men lining up to use my ass. Oh god, he's right. What's worse… I want it. It's the ultimate way to be a fucktoy for the night. If this cock wasn't in my mouth, I would beg for it. Would Cameron let it happen?

My head whirls and another orgasm rips through me unexpectedly. I convulse from the energy and cry out around the cock in my mouth as the dude blows his load deep in my throat. I'm beyond caring about anything, and I lap and suck on this guy's cock while holding back my gleeful whimpers as the dude in my pussy fucks me rougher than anyone has ever fucked me.

When he shoves my knees to my chest, I welcome the position change. The angle makes the pleasure sharper as ecstasy courses through my body. The room fills with a chorus of moans and groans, and I'm chanting "Fuck me" as the guy removes his cock from my mouth. Within moments, the guy between my legs deposits his load of cum in my pussy as he growls out with his release.

Cameron grips my chin and turns my face towards him as he kisses me deeply, sucking at my lips and tongue that just cleaned off the other guy's cum. Oh hell, that's hot.

It barely registers when another guy climbs on the bed, and he keeps my knees up to my chest as he drills into my pussy. I thought the first guy was huge, but this new guy makes the first guy seem small. I groan as he stretches my pussy beyond anything I've ever felt before. It's a painful pleasure that I welcome. I never want this guy to stop fucking me.

I scream out a stream of obscenities as the dude hammers at my pussy. The delight is too intense, and I explode around his cock within a minute.

"Ohhhh, fuuuuuck," I scream as I come apart.

My pussy squeezes around him as he fucks me furiously, each thrust sending a heavy pair of balls whacking against my ass. A dangerous, alarming desire flits along the edge of my consciousness. I don't know that I want this to be only one time. This is so fucking incredible.

The gigantic dude in my pussy roars and paints my cave walls with load after load of hot cum. I'm a bundle of lust and desperate for more. I'm not surprised when he's immediately replaced with another guy. How many guys have fucked me? I think it was two in my mouth, and three or four in my pussy... If it's four, that means someone is coming back for more. A fuzziness washes over me when I realize they could keep using me like this for hours.

Cameron whispers, "I love you," and gets up on his knees. The familiar scent of him fills me as he pushes his cock between my lips and fucks my mouth at the exact pace and depth he knows I can withstand. He's the roughest of them, and I welcome his thrusts in my throat as the new guy in my pussy fucks me with abandon.

Someone's finger is on my clit, and I whimper around Cameron's cock as I edge close to another orgasm. Holy fuck, how many is this now? I try to count as I come again; this one is almost painful in intensity. They seem to build on each other, and as the blast overwhelms me, I scream out and stop thinking all together.

I'm floating in a daze and barely notice that Cameron doesn't come before he pulls out. Every inch of my body is teased and played with.

When someone fingers my ass, Cameron growls, "Stop. That's mine someday." The guy quickly removes his hand.

It's possible hours pass. Time has no meaning, but eventually the room goes silent as everyone but Cameron leaves. He tugs the blindfold off, and I blink in the soft lighting. He covers me and slides his cock between my sore and used folds as the soft joy surprises me.

He fucks me slowly and passionately, mixing all the men's cum with my juices as he drives his cock into my wet hole. He kisses me and murmurs that he loves me. I'm beyond coming again, but I welcome his orgasm when he finally climaxes with a groan.

He collapses on me and kisses my neck while I relax into the bed, totally spent.

"Steph, you were perfect and so goddamn lovely."

I try to lift an arm to caress his back, but I have no energy.

He twists off me. "You need a drink."

He helps me sit up, and a bottle of cool water touches my lips. I sip greedily, and after he sets it on the nightstand, he helps me nibble on some crackers he'd brought upstairs for this purpose.

The snack and water revive me a little, but I'm utterly exhausted and more in love with my husband than I've ever been in our entire marriage. This night was magnificent, and Cameron made it that way.

We snuggle, facing one another, and he brushes his thumb across my cheek. "Steph, you okay?"

I yawn and giggle. "Oh, yeah. I just need sleep... Was everyone pleased?"

He kisses my forehead. "Oh yeah, you definitely pleased them all. Now sleep, my princess, we can talk more in the morning."

I smile, already partway asleep. "Cameron?" I mumble.

"Yes, baby?"

I can tell I'm about to zonk out, but I want him to know something first. "Think it's time for you to claim my ass."

He laughs at that and pulls me closer to him. "Oh yeah, you're going to beg for it first. We'll talk about that in the morning as well."

"Sounds good," I mutter and fall asleep.

The End

GRATIFYING THE GUYS

CHAPTER 1

The smell of bacon lures me towards the kitchen while my mouth waters. My husband, Sebastian, woke up before me, and he's creating the delicious aroma throughout the house. Since he's going to the gym today, I didn't expect him to make breakfast — and definitely not bacon, since we usually only have it on the days we're staying home and being couch potatoes.

I'm happy he's still home, and I pull at the neckline of my t-shirt and bounce in my sneakers as I stroll into the kitchen. I've got an abundance of excess energy this morning, and I figured Sebastian had already left for the gym, so I'd planned to get a quick run in while he was gone. Now all I want to do is attack a pile of bacon and skip the run.

Sebastian's facing away from me, and I get a sexy view of his tight ass in his gray boxer briefs. All he's wearing are boxers and an apron.

Lust simmers in my gut as I press against him, fondle his buns, and kiss the back of his neck. "What's up, buttercup?"

I squeeze each ass cheek, and he moans, "You hungry?"

He asks as if he didn't already know he was going to share. We've been together six years now, and I don't think I've ever turned down bacon. I peek around his shoulder and he's dishing up two plates with scrambled eggs and toast. Mmm, yeah, that looks tasty, but so does his cute butt. It's a toss-up which I want more.

"I'm *starving*," I tease, exaggerating my words. "But *not* for food."

He laughs, moves out of my grasp, and carries the plates to the table. "Jasmine — babydoll — behave. We have a busy day."

I follow him and notice he'd already set glasses of water down for us before I got to the kitchen.

I fake grumble as I sit down. "Why did two of our friends choose the same weekend to get married?"

I'm not expecting him to answer, and he kisses my forehead before taking a seat and ravenously attacking his eggs and bacon. He doesn't seem interested in a quick fuck this morning. Bummer. Every Friday we usually fool around and fall asleep in a tangle of sweaty limbs, but that didn't happen last night. Vanessa, one of my closest friends, got married, and I was a bridesmaid with duties that kept me busy. By the time we got home from the wedding, we were exhausted and crashed.

We have another wedding to attend tonight, but thankfully I'm not in the bridal party. The plan is to drag Sebastian to the dance floor and grind against him long enough to convince him to cut out early. It's been a long week of no nookie. I'm working on my doctorate degree in psychology, so between my schooling and him working, this babydoll needs to get stuffed tonight.

I eat slowly, watching him in my peripheral vision. I want to untie that silly apron, climb into his lap, and go to town on Willy — the pet name I gave his cock because it makes me giggle every time I say it.

"Did you like the wedding last night?" he asks.

I shrug. "It was fun. Vanessa and Mason looked happy."

I take a sip of water and almost spit it out at his next question.

"Do you know what freeuse is?" he asks casually, like he just heard about a new trend on social media.

My mind goes blank. I know exactly what it is from Vanessa and my other friend, Nadia, but what does he know about it?

"Um, yes... But I've never done it or even thought of doing it, so..."

Yeah, that's a lie. As soon as Nadia told me she and her husband had been messing around with freeuse weekends, I researched the kink. I've been fantasizing about doing it with Sebastian. I'm just so dang busy, I don't have time to give up a weekend to let him use me whenever he wants.

He shovels the last bite of egg into his mouth and gets up to put his dirty dishes in the sink. When he comes back to the table, he leans in, his lips mere inches from my ear, and he speaks softly. "Would you like to be my freeuse slut?"

His breath on my neck sends a shiver through me and I match the tone of his voice, whispering, "Yes."

I'm not done eating, but the food is all but forgotten as I tilt my head up. He searches my face, as if he's trying to determine whether I'm serious. A low hum of desire burns in me. I'll do whatever it takes to get his wonderful cock inside me today. He peers down at my chest and then back up, making me fidget.

"The guys were talking about it at the wedding. Can we try it today?" he asks hoarsely.

Knowing he was probably talking to Nadia's husband, and possibly the groomsmen from last night who fucked Vanessa, gives me a rush. I've heard the tales from the women's side of the story, and I wonder what their hubbies told Sebastian. Not that it matters, as long as he fucks me.

My voice sounds breathy when I answer. "Yes, but only today. I have classwork to finish tomorrow."

Even as I tell him I'm busy, I know that if he woke me up tomorrow morning by fucking me, I'd lie there, loving it.

He kisses my temple. "Then finish eating so I can use you."

I grin and take a big bite of egg, chewing dramatically. I expect him to go do something else, but he stays where he is, watching me like a hawk. A flush creeps up my neck, and it's difficult to swallow. Is he going to stand there the entire time? It seems like he's toying with me, and my pussy throbs in response to remind me we enjoy being toyed with.

There's no way I'm going to finish my food, so I stand up and push my chair in. He'll probably drag me to the bedroom as soon as I set the plate in the sink. Before I can pick up my dishes, he steps behind me and applies pressure to my shoulder, forcing me to bend over the table, directly onto my dirty plate. Uh, what the fuck?

He removes the glass of water and sets it on the counter, and I stay smooshed into the plate. This is a new experience. He's never shoved me into food before. Is this even sexy?

When he comes back, he forces his hardness against my ass. His hands slide under my shirt around the sides, and he lifts me up a little and cups my breasts through my sports bra. Okay, I take it back. This is hot. I whimper, and my pussy lights up as he removes his hands from my shirt and presses me back down onto the wooden surface. Why is this turning me on?

I wiggle against one of his hands as he skims it over my stretch pants and rubs between my legs. I gasp when he spanks me, hard, and the sharp pleasure makes me tingle.

"Don't move. Pretend like I'm not doing anything."

Um... I'm squished against my unfinished breakfast, and I'm supposed to pretend nothing out of the ordinary is going on?

He nudges his cock against my ass again and I arch my back and moan loudly, "Please."

When he slaps my ass again, I whimper. Oh shit! He's gonna do it again. My body trembles as anticipation builds.

"Babydoll, you don't seem to understand. You're my fucktoy today, and I told you to pretend nothing is going on."

Desire ripples through me. I think too much all the time, and the rare occasions I can let go and become a fucktoy are amazing. Maybe freeuse will get me in the right mindset to shut my brain off.

His fingers slip into the waistband of my pants and panties and drag them down. He only gets them as far as my knees before stopping. I'm still wearing my running shoes, so getting them off my feet would have been a challenge. I moan from arousal as he slides his hand between my legs and rubs my clit.

He presses two fingers into my pussy. "Do you realize the power you gave me today?"

I moan louder, but don't answer.

He continues. "I'm going to use you whenever I want, however I want, wherever I want, and you're going to just take it."

Oh, fuck, that's hot. My head spins as he finger fucks me roughly. Spikes of bliss swirl in my stomach, and I peep out in distress when he pulls his hand away. Dammit, it was just getting good.

He tugs on my shoulder, indicating he wants me to stand, and the plate sticks to my shirt for a moment and clatters to the table as I rise. My shirt is a fucking mess, and I almost laugh while he turns me around to face him. He lifts my chin with his hand and stares at me intensely as he steps close enough that his cock presses against my stomach. While I was bent over, he removed the apron and pulled his boxers down far enough to free Willy, and his skin is warm and smooth.

Sebastian crushes his lips to mine, and I open up and welcome his seeking tongue. He holds me against him, kissing me with such passion, and I feel dizzy from the lack of oxygen.

When he breaks off the kiss, he says, "You are a freeuse slut. Now say it."

I nod as a shimmer of yearning grips me. I need his cock so badly.

"Say it," he commands.

"I'm a freeuse slut."

"Good girl."

I almost moan at his approval. I glance over my shoulder at the mess we made of the table and squeal when he picks me up and sets me on the edge. He removes my sneakers, one by one, dropping them to the floor with a thud, and pulls my pants and panties off the rest of the way.

"Put your foot on the chair and spread your legs," he orders, and I immediately obey.

I'm usually the dominant one in our sexual play, and I'm loving this side of him. Who knew my sweet buttercup had a tiger lurking in him?

He rubs my clit with his fingers again, and I cry out. I'm already wet and desperate for him. He pushes two fingers inside me, and I jerk against him, aching for more. He pushes my knees further apart and removes his hand, replacing it with the tip of his cock. As he sinks into me, my body instinctively clenches around him.

"Oh god!"

He grins wickedly at my reaction. "Does my freeuse slut like this?"

Calling me his freeuse slut and not by my name sinks me further into the mindset I crave.

"Yes," I groan as I grip the edge of the table and rotate my hips, trying to rub his shaft against my cave walls.

He pushes me down until I'm on my back as he strokes in and out. My dirty plate is half under me, but I don't care. My whole body is buzzing as pleasure builds in my core, and I whimper with each movement.

He grabs ahold of my hips as he speeds up and starts talking dirty.

"Does my fucktoy like this?" He doesn't give me time to respond as he hammers against me. "Your pussy feels so damn good."

I moan, "Yes."

"Is my slut ready to come?"

I squeeze my eyes shut and hold on to the edge of the table firmly, rocking my hips with every deep plunge of his cock.

I'm so close, and when he thrusts harder, I moan, "Yesssss," in one long breath. I don't want him to stop, and I chant "Fuck me" as my thigh muscles tense, welcoming the bliss.

He's fucking me so hard, the table squeaks, and my sighs and moans join his panting as I spiral higher and higher.

I'm almost lost in delight when he says, "Come for me, babydoll."

I scream out, "Oh... my... god!" as my orgasm rips through me.

My heart is racing as I luxuriate in the sweet sensation. A few more strokes later, he groans and his cock twitches while he blows his load. He shudders and pumps into me as I drift in a haze of sexual delight. When he pulls out, I take a few seconds to realize he's done with me.

I lift my lashes and he's gazing down at me with love.

"Wow," I murmur softly.

"Babydoll, this is only the beginning. I've got all day to use you."

Desire races through my veins as I grin at him. "Sounds good to me."

He helps me to a sitting position and kisses my forehead. "I'm going to get cleaned up and go to the gym. Be a good girl while I'm gone."

As he leaves the kitchen, I study his sexy, naked ass, and cheerfully call out, "Aye aye, Captain."

My pussy throbs with the aftermath of my climax. Well, hell, if freeuse includes me having orgasms, I'm down for this every Friday or Saturday. Heck, we could call it Freeuse Friday. Mmm, yeah.

The food smeared across the table catches my attention, and I look down at my t-shirt and can't hold in my bark of laughter. Okay, I need to clean up the kitchen and shower. I'm one filthy slut.

CHAPTER 2

I tidy the kitchen and pop in a piece of spearmint gum from a pack on the counter. When Sebastian comes in to give me a quick kiss on his way out the door to the gym, he murmurs, "Mmm, minty," and tries to steal the gum from my mouth. Laughing, I swat him away. God, I love that goofball.

Taking my time in the shower, I daydream about how many times he's going to use me today. He usually comes home from the gym horny, so I bet I get it at least one more time before the wedding. Once I'm out of the shower and dry, I toss on my favorite sundress and prowl around the house with excess energy. I need to find something to do before Sebastian gets home since all I can think about is him walking in the door and bending me over the nearest surface.

When my phone rings, I see it's my best friend Stephanie calling, and I smile as I answer.

"Yo, bitch. What's up?"

I purposely pop my gum in her ear, hoping she laughs at me. When she says I'm never going to believe the morning she's had, I plop down on the couch. Oh, hell yeah, this is just the distraction I need. I'm still daydreaming about Sebastian coming home and fucking me, and I almost miss it when she tells me that her husband is going to have her fuck all his basketball friends tonight.

I screech, "No fucking way!" into the phone, and she sounds amused by my reaction.

What the hell? She's now my third friend who is doing a freeuse day that turned into some slutty gangbang. My pussy buzzes, and I space out, daydreaming about being double stuffed. Shit, that's hot. Where's my gangbang offer? I hold in a snort. No way in hell Sebastian would ever go for that, and I don't really need it since I'm having fun with this freeuse thing.

Stephanie and I chat for a bit. She sounds insecure about whether she's doing the right thing, and I assure her it's fine. Why didn't the guys tell Sebastian how wonderful it was to have their wife fuck a bunch of other dudes? Why focus only on the freeuse part? My pussy throbs again, and I rub my thighs together. Yeah, I need to stop thinking about a bunch of guys using me like a fucktoy. This is a quick road to nowhere.

I'm filling Stephanie in on the details of my kitchen romp when I hear Sebastian get home. Heck yeah, fun times are about to begin again.

I rush into the phone, "Ohhh, I gotta go. I just heard the garage door. Love you!" I disconnect the call right as Sebastian walks into the living room.

I grin at him. "Hi, sweet cheeks."

He comes over for a kiss. "Hi, babydoll. Did you miss me?"

"I missed you *soooo* much. I almost died of loneliness."

He sits on the couch next to me, and I rest against him.

"Hah, somehow I doubt it."

When he turns the TV on, I toss him the side-eye. Why isn't he fucking me yet?

"Did you get a good workout?"

He rolls his shoulders as he chooses a stand-up comedy show to stream. "I did. I'll be sore tomorrow, but it was worth it."

Hmm... fine, I guess we'll watch TV. We only have a couple of hours before we have to get ready for the wedding. But if it's his freeuse day, I have to just let him do whatever he wants... even if it isn't doing me. I cuddle closer to him, and he tugs me up into his lap so I'm sitting sideways with my legs stretched out along the cushions. A thrill runs through me. Ohhh, maybe I'm wrong, and he's going for it. He wraps his arms around me, pulling me close, and I feel him relax.

I wait expectantly for a solid minute, but he gets engrossed in the show. Ugh, fuck. Laying my head on his shoulder, I nuzzle his neck and breathe in deeply, taking in his scent. Some people find it odd when I say it, but I love the smell of Sebastian when he gets home from the gym. I try not to geek out on people about the psychology of how the scent of your partner relaxes you, but the quirks of the brain amaze me. But no matter the reason, if he comes home sweaty, I love cuddling with him as long as I can shower before I leave the house.

I give him a couple of neck kisses and turn my attention to the show. It's not my favorite comedian, but it's still funny, and I get sucked in and giggle along with Sebastian's deep laughs. I'm comfortable and don't pay attention to his hand tracing slow circles on my bare shoulder. The sundress I'm wearing leaves my shoulders and arms bare, so he has clear access to rub the length of my arm up to my neck.

After several minutes of stroking my skin, he repositions his legs and my ass comes into contact with his growing erection. I notice him glance down the valley of my cleavage and then back up to the TV. Well, well, well, he's not uninterested after all. My stomach flutters at the thought.

Sebastian's hand moves between my shoulder blades and traces the length of my spine. As his fingers trail down my back through the fabric of my dress, I shiver, and a gush of wetness hits my panties. This better be going in the direction I think it is. He keeps one hand on my back and places his other on my thigh. His fingers creep up my leg, giving me goosebumps, and I shift my body slightly to spread my legs wider and give him better access.

When he says, "Don't stop watching," my mind goes fuzzy as I try to concentrate on the show.

He moves his hand up, rubbing me through my panties, and I hold in a moan as my vision glazes over. Does he really expect me to watch the TV? I gasp when his fingers slide underneath the band of my panties to tease my slit, dipping inside my folds and sliding back out. I can't help myself; I try to grind against his hand.

"Babydoll, what are you doing?"

His tone says I'm misbehaving, so I peek up at him. He's watching the show, but I need him to fuck me, so I don't care if I'm being bad. He's hard enough, so I'm confident he's going to give me what I want no matter what I do.

I'm flippant in my reply. "I think you know."

The corners of his mouth twitch and he presses his lips to my hair. "You're such a naughty girl."

I writhe and moan, "Yes, now please fuck me."

Without looking away from the TV, he bounces me in his lap, causing his cock to rub against my pussy, and I moan louder.

His chuckle vibrates against my ear. "Keep that up, and I won't."

"Please, just fuck me already," I whimper in frustration.

"Tell me what you want, babydoll."

Didn't I just tell him? I shimmy my hips. "Fuck me, please."

"I think you forgot something. This isn't about what you want. Now keep watching the show."

Oh, fuck. I press my lips together to contain a whine and pretend to watch the show. He continues to bounce me in his lap, and I hold in my gasps and ignore the need to grind against him. Within a few minutes, I can't take much more of the torture. What sort of shitty freeuse day is this? Isn't he supposed to use me?

"Stand up a moment," he demands, and I'm disoriented as I do what he asks.

He takes his cock out of his sweatpants, slides his hands up the sides of my hips, and yanks my panties down. Mmm, yeah, this is getting good. They fall to the floor and I step out of them as he tugs me back into his lap, positioning me straight onto his cock. The tip slides inside me and gravity takes over, bringing me down until I'm balls deep.

"Ohhhh, god," I moan as delight ripples through me.

"Now watch the show, babydoll. This isn't about your enjoyment."

Fuck. Did the guys at the wedding tell him to treat me this way, or is this natural for him? I'm loving it, and keep my eyes trained on the TV as he holds onto my hips and forces me to rotate against his cock. I keep my hands in my lap, trying to pretend I'm not doing anything out of the ordinary. A small part of me feels like a dirty little whore from how he's treating me, and it turns me on even more. I shiver with excitement and bite my lip. I'm going to come soon at this rate.

Sebastian flexes his hips, speeding up his thrusts. Since he's not letting me move, he's staying fully sheathed, and the tip of his cock massages the pleasure points deep in my pussy. It's driving me wilder than if he was doing long strokes in and out.

The bliss builds, and I finally crack, wiggling against him with a groan. I undulate against his cock, trying to get him deeper inside me. The friction causes me to cry out loudly. I'm almost there. Just another minute.

He must be able to tell I'm about to climax because he wraps my hair around his fist, pulls my head up, and growls, "Watch the show, babydoll! Don't you dare come!"

Shit. I cry out again, and I quiver in anticipation as he thrusts harder and faster. He pulls me down against him until he's slamming into me. I feel his cock twitch right before he explodes. Ohhh, fuck... I haven't come!

He groans and pumps his seed deep inside me, and I whimper when the pleasure ends abruptly. I sag back onto his lap, and my pussy spasms from the denied orgasm. I'm crazy turned on and in shock that it's over. He lets go of my hair and rests his forehead on my back, sighing softly.

"Are you okay?" he murmurs into my hair.

"Yeah, but... I didn't finish," I whisper.

He lifts his head, brushes my hair to the side, and kisses the back of my neck. "I know, babydoll. But this is freeuse. Do you want to stop?"

I frown and look down at my hands, confused, and I'm not sure how I want to answer. "Am I going to come again today?"

He's quiet for a minute, as if he's thinking. "I'll tell you what, let's make a deal."

What's this? I perk up as he continues.

"I want you to do your old bimbo routine at the wedding tonight and get a bunch of guys panting after you. Then I'll bring you home and fuck you so hard you'll see stars."

I'm nodding before he even finishes, and my pussy clenches around his softening shaft. "Deal."

CHAPTER 3

The rest of the afternoon is a blur of activity as we both shower and get ready for the wedding. I planned to wear comfortable shoes to dance in, but now that I need guys drooling over me, I switch them out for some sexy, spiked heels. My dress is a gray, form-fitting number with a thigh slit; my toned runner's legs are one of my best features, so the dress looks amazing on me. I keep my long, platinum-blonde hair down in soft waves, and I'm extra careful with my makeup. When I'm done, I look and feel sexy.

In my early 20s, I used to get my kicks out of making guys think I was a bimbo. Sometimes I just wanted mindless sex and would choose a hot jock who looked like he was good for a night of fun, never letting on that everything I was doing was calculated to get him to fuck me. When we were done — usually a seedy encounter in a dirty bathroom — he thought he just scored with a hot bimbo, and I was content from my orgasm. I didn't realize what I was doing was a kink until later when I was researching a college project.

The funniest part is that it led me to Sebastian. He was one of my filthy bathroom conquests, but after he fucked me against the wall and gave me a mind-blowing orgasm, he turned apologetic like he had just done the most horrible thing ever by losing control. He was an adorable, lost puppy, but as soon as he started spiraling and said something about how he took advantage of me, I dropped the bimbo act. We ended up talking for hours at a bar, and we've been together ever since.

Occasionally, for fun, I pretend to be a bimbo again with him, and I found out that sex is more fulfilling when the person doesn't really think of you that way and you both know it's just an act. And hey, it keeps the spice alive. He's never asked me to act this way towards other people though, so tonight is something different. My pussy is still buzzing from the lack of orgasms, so I'm going to do whatever it takes to get that hard fucking, and I better see those stars he promised.

The wedding ceremony is beautiful and sentimental, but Sebastian's fingers caressing the skin of my thigh exposed by the slit in my dress distracts me the entire time. It's amusing that all the guests seem to be the same people we keep seeing at all these weddings. We're just one big group of friends, and only the relatives change. It already seems like eons ago, but Vanessa's wedding was only last night. Mason and Vanessa are off on some fancy, tropical honeymoon, but the rest of the wedding party is here.

Knowing that the groomsmen fucked her last night, I study them curiously. I wonder how many times they all came. Hell, how many times did SHE come? With that many cocks plowing into her, I'd guess it was at least three or four times. Maybe some of them came over her. Ooooh, maybe it turned into a circle jerk with her on the floor. Fuck, that's hot, especially if she was in her wedding dress. I twist in my seat, trying to find some relief for the ache between my legs, and I can tell that I'm flushed. It's not from the crowded, warm room, but if anyone noticed, they might think it was.

When the ceremony ends, people get up to head into the hotel's reception hall, but Sebastian leans over and whispers in my ear. "You seemed a little worked up during the ceremony. What were you thinking about?"

My brain freezes, and my lips part. Do I tell him I was thinking about a circle jerk and wondering how many orgasms Vanessa had last night? I'm not sure he's ready to hear every filthy thought in my head, so I shrug and play it cool. "Nothing."

He shoots me a roguish grin. "No, it wasn't nothing. If you want to come tonight, you'll tell me."

Ugh. I could lie... fuck it, why bother? I turn towards him, give a slow smile, and this time it's me who moves in close to his ear. I kiss his earlobe, and gently tug the flesh between my teeth, knowing it makes him shiver.

My breath is a soft puff when I purr. "I was imagining a circle jerk of men ejaculating on me."

He pulls back and gapes at me. "Were they jerking each other off, or only themselves?"

I have to hold in my laugh. That's the first thing that pops into his head?

"I wasn't paying attention. I was waiting for the splashes of cum to coat me."

He looks like he's digesting the thought, and then he shrugs. "I bet they were only touching themselves."

Oh my God, his wife says she's daydreaming about a group of guys coming all over her, and all he can think about is whether the dudes are crossing swords? Shit, this is why I love him.

I slide my hand into his and squeeze it. "Sweet cheeks, let's go dance, so I can play the bimbo and get fucked hard."

He stands and gives me an answering grin. "I just needed a moment to process. Come to find out, I married a slut who wants to be covered in cum."

I laugh loudly. "Oh honey..." I pull him towards the exit. "I haven't even told you about my double-stuff fantasy from earlier. You married a super slut."

The reception has barely started, but I excuse myself and leave Sebastian at a table while I follow a pack of women to the restroom. I'm not watching where I'm going and run into someone coming out of the bathroom.

I wobble and almost tip into the wall, blindly apologizing. "Oh shit, I'm sorry!"

A light, feminine laugh that I'd recognize anywhere rings out. "Don't worry about it, Jasmine. I'm impressed you can walk in those heels."

Millie, one of my close friends, grins at me. She was another one of Vanessa's bridesmaids. I hadn't noticed she was here tonight, despite knowing she planned to attend. She and her husband must have been sitting behind us.

I rotate my leg to show off the thigh slit and my sexy shoes. "I'm seducing Sebastian tonight. This outfit is my secret weapon."

"Somehow I doubt you need much help to seduce him." She laughs again, and I lower my voice.

"We're playing with a freeuse day."

She tilts her head and raises an eyebrow. "That's different from usual?"

"Yep. I'm going to put on a bimbo show to get him worked up, and then he can fuck me as hard as he wants." I smile at her. "It should be interesting."

Her brow furrows slightly. "Well, I hope you get your orgasm. Freeuse sounds fun for the user, but not so much for the usee."

I giggle. "Yeah, I already didn't come once today. I'm banking on me being so turned on that I explode as soon as he fucks me again."

I can tell she's puzzled as we say goodbye. Not everyone understands the appeal of being used like a sex toy, and that's fine. It's good I didn't mention the circle jerk fantasy.

After a glass of wine and a slow dance of rubbing against Sebastian, he pulls me off the dance floor and out to a quiet side hallway. He kisses me softly, and I sway towards him. This is nice, but I can't spend all night snogging him. I haven't found an opportunity yet to follow his instructions.

"Don't you want me to flirt with other guys?"

"Mmm, yes. I want you to be my horny slut tonight, so I'm working you up."

God, why do I love it so much when he calls me filthy things?

Leaning in, I give him a hard kiss. "Then let's go back to the party so I can slut it up."

He laughs. "One thing first. I'm going to sit and watch you flirt with other guys, but while you're doing it, I want you to think about the guy standing over you and jerking off."

All thoughts drain from my head while I stare at him and blink. When I can think again, my senses buzz alive with a whoosh. My nipples pucker, and I feel myself growing more wet. My entire body tingles. Holy fuck, that's dirty and I love it.

He must be able to tell he stunned me for a moment because he laughs again and kisses my nose. "Can you do that for me?"

I nod. Fuck yeah, I can. "It's going to be rough, but a girl's gotta do what a girl's gotta do."

He cups my ass and squeezes it. "Go find someone to flirt with while I visit the restroom."

Nodding and smiling, I take a deep breath and turn away from him to go find a potential flirt-buddy.

Once I'm out of his sight, I run into Cameron and Stephanie leaving early. She's living her best life because I know she is having sex with a bunch of guys tonight. I'm having fun with Sebastian and this playful side of him, but would he ever consider sharing me? I think I need to ease him into the idea. He's the type of guy who likes to think about things for a while and isn't one to jump headfirst into anything... unless it's fucking a bimbo in the bathroom years ago, but even then, he felt horrible afterwards.

I down another glass of wine and grab the closest cute guy I can find to dance with. The next hour is a blur of flirting and dancing, but I'm hyper aware of all the guys looking at me. I'm attracting interest because of my outfit and how free I am with my attention. I make sure that every time I dance with a guy, it's within Sebastian's view from the table where he's sitting, and I purposely touch the men's shoulders or brush against them as we're dancing. None of the guys seem aware of what I'm doing, which is fine with me, but the longer it goes on, the more Sebastian looks hot under the collar. He's getting turned on by this, and knowing that gets me even more excited. It's an amusing feedback loop of eroticism.

I'm dancing with one of Sebastian's closest friends, Brian, when I realize my husband isn't sitting and watching me anymore. Where did he go? I look around the crowd of people and spot him resting against the wall near one exit, talking with two guys. Both of them are wearing suits. They look familiar, but their backs are to me so I can't tell who they are at first. Oh wait, I know who they are. They're the groomsmen who fucked Vanessa last night.

A vision of them spurting cum all over her makes my heart race, and I feel my face heat. It seems fucked up to be picturing my friend getting jizzed on. I plan on asking her how she liked her night with the guys the next time I talk to her, and hopefully I don't run off at the mouth and ask whether she was covered in cum in the end.

I'm distracted by my naughty thoughts when Brian and I stop dancing. I step away, smiling at him, and as we weave through the crowd of couples dancing, my gaze drifts past him. It lands on the two groomsmen. Dang, they're handsome guys. Vanessa got lucky.

One of them — David — turns to look at me, and his eyes meet mine. His mouth splits into a wide grin, and I'm immediately paranoid. What is Sebastian telling them? Is he saying that I'm his freeuse slut tonight?

I hope he is.

My breathing quickens. Is this crazy? I want my husband to spread it around that I'm his freeuse slut. I probably need therapy. Just because I'm getting a doctorate in psychology doesn't mean I'm not just as messed up as the next person.

I watch them talk for a moment, and I daydream again. This time it's not Vanessa getting covered in cum. It's me. Yeah… I'm such a slut. I'm getting turned on even more thinking about my husband sharing me.

David's mouth moves like he's saying something to Sebastian, but he keeps his eyes glued to mine. He beams a smile at me, and when I smile back, he turns to Sebastian and the other guy. I try to focus on Brian, but I can't stop staring at the men talking to Sebastian. My legs tremble, making me wobble in my shoes.

"Jasmine, you okay?" Brian's hand touches my arm, and he pulls me out of my perverted trance.

I think the wine and dancing got to my head because I shake my head and blurt out, "I was just daydreaming about my husband sharing me with other guys."

"Oh." He frowns and rubs his chin. "I didn't know you guys had an open marriage."

"We don't…" I let my voice trail off.

He sighs and I can tell he's disappointed. "Guess Sebastian gets you all to himself tonight."

Wait, what? This is Sebastian's best friend. My mouth flops open like a fish, and I don't know how to respond. Brian wishes he could fuck me? But… But… What? Did Sebastian say something to him?

I glance over at Sebastian, who is still talking with his friends. He's animated, and his eyes sparkle. He looks like he's having a great conversation. God, I need to sit down.

Brian follows me as I beeline to the nearest table and slide into a chair.

"Are you okay?" he asks.

I wave him off. "I'm fine, just a little tipsy."

He looks towards Sebastian. "If you're sure you're fine, I'm going to go talk with the guys."

I tell him to go have fun, and I rest my elbow on the table and put my chin in my hand. This night has taken a very odd turn. I feel like a voyeur, watching my husband and wondering what they're all saying. I'm secretly hoping it's about me and my sluttiness. I mean, I have been fantasizing about him sharing me with other guys. It's not like it'll really happen, so why does it feel so wrong in a deliciously naughty way?

I'm still daydreaming when Sebastian joins me. He bends down, gives me a deep kiss, and pulls me to my feet.

"Jasmine, I've got a new offer for you."

I tilt my head back in surprise. "What?"

"If you really want a bunch of guys to come all over you, I have volunteers."

My pussy clenches, and a ripple of desire swirls low in my belly. I shake my head. Fuck, I'm dreaming and just imagined Sebastian offering to share me.

When I don't reply, a huge grin spreads across his face, and he raises his eyebrows suggestively at me. "Come on, Jasmine. You said you wanted a bunch of guys to cover you with cum, right?"

A blush creeps up my face. Did I actually say that, or did I tell him I was imagining Vanessa covered in cum? Shit, now I don't remember. Obviously, he understood I was thinking about myself.

I nod but say nothing. I'm too flabbergasted by the turn of events, and I don't want to admit how much I want him to share me in case he's teasing me.

He leans closer, and I can smell the cologne he wears. It smells masculine and spicy.

He holds my waist and pulls me towards him. "Say it, Jasmine. Say you want my friends to cover you with cum."

His breath tickles my neck, and I shiver.

"Yes," I whisper. "I want your friends to come all over me."

Sebastian croons, "Good slut," and kisses me softly. "You've been a good girl tonight. I think you deserve a reward."

I like the way he's thinking. He pulls me out of the room, into the hallway, and keeps walking. Where is he taking me?

He pauses in front of a door. "Babydoll, my friends are waiting on the other side of this door. Do you really want this?"

I swallow hard. My heart races and my skin tingles. I want this so badly.

"Yes, please." I squeeze his arm and nod.

His eyes crinkle with amusement. "Do you want more than a circle jerk?"

My mouth forms an O. Uh... I take a few seconds to reply. "What do you mean, more?"

He licks his lips and grins wickedly. "I've been imagining watching them fuck you. Free pass tonight. Do you want it?"

Holy shit! "Just for tonight, right? This changes nothing?"

That makes him laugh. "Oh, it changes something. I'm going to have an amazing memory to jack off to."

This seems crazy and totally unlike him. Who knows if he'll ever be in this mood again. Fuck it, I'm not passing up this chance.

"I'm game if you are."

He kisses my nose. "As long as I get to watch them fuck you, I'm game."

Oh, I'm totally on board with this. I take his hand and squeeze it. "Bring it on."

CHAPTER 4

Four guys wait in the room for us: Brian, David, David's twin brother, Leo, and their other friend, Aaron. I hadn't seen Aaron at the reception, so I don't know how he got involved with this, but I'm not going to question my good fortune. He's gorgeous, and I always thought he seemed like a sweetheart of a guy.

The room is a fancy office with a couch along one wall. I'm fairly certain we're not supposed to be in here and I don't know how they got the key. But, again, no questions. This is better than a dirty bathroom, so I'm not one to be picky.

The guys all look at me, and I suddenly feel shy. What do I say to them? Welcome to my pussy, I hope you enjoy it? Yeah... no.

I squeak out, "Hi, guys."

Sebastian closes the door and locks it, then walks over to the desk and pulls the office chair to a corner before sitting down.

"Babydoll, give me a striptease."

He motions to me, and I walk over and stand in front of him.

"Remove your clothes."

I take a deep breath and turn, presenting my back to Sebastian so he can unzip my dress. It feels like it takes forever for him to work the zipper, and when he finally does, the sound is louder than normal. I turn back around to face him again and shrug my dress off, letting it pool on the floor before kicking it aside.

Sebastian's voice is rough. "All of them."

I unfasten my strapless bra and toss it on top of my dress. I slide my panties down, bending over to step out of them carefully because I still have my high heels on. The men behind me are getting a very graphic view of my wet pussy, and it makes me feel like even more of a slut.

I'm naked except for my shoes. I stand up straight, waiting to see if he tells me to take them off as well. He doesn't.

"Turn around." His voice is deep and powerful.

This feels so naughty, but I love it. Turning around, I face the other men and shake my ass at Sebastian. He fondles me for a moment.

"Damn, babydoll, you're so fucking sexy. Now go suck on David's cock."

A delicious hunger for the forbidden quickens my pulse at his words. Fuuuuck, that's hot.

David sits down on the couch and unzips his pants, pulling his cock out. I can't fucking believe I'm about to suck off one of Sebastian's friends. I kneel between David's legs and grip the base of his shaft, hovering my mouth over the tip. David presses my head down gently, and I fit my lips around his cock, needing no further encouragement. His shaft is pleasantly thick, and I waste no time getting into it as I bob up and down on him, sucking greedily, making sure everyone sees me deep-throating his cock.

I hear one guy groan, and it makes me more excited. For all I know, this could just be a normal weekend night for them all, but this is something I've never done before, and the experience is surreal. When I woke up this morning, I never imagined the evening would end this way.

I suck him for a while, and he moves his hips, fucking my throat.

"Fuck yeah, Jasmine. You're so good." David's voice is husky, and I can hear the excitement in his tone.

I moan around his cock, loving the feel of him in my mouth. As I suck him, I rub the base of his shaft with one hand and slip my other hand between my legs. I'm dripping wet, and I groan as my fingers find my clit. I'm desperate to come, but the party just started.

Sebastian calls out, "I think someone needs to fuck her while she's being such a good girl sucking on David."

My body stiffens from shock at his words, and I catch movement out of the corner of my eye as Aaron moves behind me, kneeling down. I hear clothes rustle and a zipper. Oh fuck, this really is going to happen. My pussy clenches and I moan louder around David's cock.

I can't believe I'm going to be fucked by another man in front of my husband. Aaron caresses my ass, and I stop rubbing my clit and reposition my knees to spread open further for him.

David grabs the back of my head and fucks my face as Aaron pulls my hips towards him. He reaches through my legs and slips his fingers inside me, pumping slowly. I whimper and swirl my tongue around the cock in my mouth. I'm so close to coming, but I need more.

"Fucking hell, you're so wet," he says.

Aaron slides his fingers out of me and reaches to the front of me to grab my tits. He squeezes them roughly, and I cry out around the shaft in my throat.

"I'm going to fuck you now." He runs his fingers through my hair and pulls my head back, forcing me to release David's cock from my mouth. Shit, I thought Aaron was going to be the gentle one.

"Ohhh god, yes." I try to move my hips towards him, wanting his cock in me.

Aaron lets go of my hair, holds onto my hips, and with one swift thrust, he impales me. Aaron's cock is huge — bigger than I expect — and I scream in surprise when intense pleasure rockets through me as he stretches me apart.

"Fuck yeah, Jasmine." He pounds into me harder, and I affix my lips around David's cock again.

I want to be spit-roasted and ping-ponged between them. I want to be ridden hard and taken by all the men. I want to be used like a cocksleeve. And in the end, I want them to jerk off on me. Fuck, I want this so bad.

David's hands are on the sides of my head, holding me still while Aaron fucks me hard and fast. I'm spinning out of control, and I can barely breathe. When Aaron slams into me extra hard, a rush of elation floods me as I climax.

"Oh fuck!" I scream, but it's garbled by David's cock.

Aaron groans and pulls out right before he comes. David releases my head and removes his cock from my mouth. Neither of them filled me with their cum. I sit up. Ugh, what is going on?

Sebastian claps. "Nice show."

I give him a questioning look over my shoulder.

He smiles. "No one gets to come until the end. They're going to use you for as long as they can and then you're going to get your wish of being covered in their cum."

I shake my head. "I'm not going to last that long."

He laughs. "That's fine. Your goal is to come as many times as you can. They're the only ones who can't."

Oh, fuck yes. Multiple orgasms for me!

Sebastian still plays director. "Get up and bend over the desk."

Yeah, I like where this is going. Luckily, the desk is mostly clear. I bend over it and give a silent apology to whoever's office this is.

"Now spread your legs wide."

I space them apart, knowing how obscene this looks. My pussy is so wet, I can feel the drops running down my inner thighs. I love how turned on I am, knowing I have four hot men lined up to use me.

Leo stands behind me and rubs my ass cheeks. "You're fucking perfect, Jasmine," he murmurs.

I whimper, enjoying his hands on my body. I've always had a soft spot in my heart for Leo. He's David's twin, but David is the fit one and Leo reminds me of just a normal dad type, albeit a pretty dang cute one.

His cock is already hard and out of his pants as he brushes it against my butt. He holds onto my ass cheeks and separates them, and I imagine he's examining me. I squirm from embarrassment. Somehow, it's worse when I think someone is inspecting my holes.

When he dips a finger into my pussy, as if he's testing my wetness, I moan and bump against him. He quickly replaces his finger with the tip of his cock, and I barely have time to register the change before he plunges his length into my eager pussy. I arch my back from the pleasure and try to hold in a groan. He grabs onto my waist as he drills into me, and I whimper as he goes deeper.

"This feels amazing," he pants.

I give a tiny nod, even though he probably can't see it, and push my butt towards him, wanting him to fuck me harder. He takes the hint, ramming into me, and I gasp as he shoves me against the desk. My nipples scrape the surface and I stretch my arms straight out so I can hold on to the far edge. My legs quiver as he hammers into my pussy, each thrust jolting me against the desk.

"Ohhh, god," I moan, and my pussy clenches around his cock as he works me into a frenzy.

I lose track of time as he uses me like the fucktoy I am. Each whack against my pussy spirals me higher and higher. The desk creaks as he slaps against me, and the other guys moan as if they're beating off while watching Leo plow into me.

I almost come from the thought, and when my husband calls out, "Come for us, babydoll," Leo's grunt and hard thrusts tip me over the edge.

My whole body shakes as I scream from the intense orgasm, and multiple guys groan with me. Leo fucks me for a bit longer before abruptly pulling out. The room tilts, and I'm lightheaded as more wetness leaks down my leg. It's only my juices since Leo didn't come.

Resting the side of my face against the surface of the desk, I wait for whoever is next. I think Brian is the only one who hasn't taken a turn with me yet, and I glance over my shoulder as he approaches. I don't have time to congratulate myself on being correct because his cock is out and pressing against my sodden hole. He slowly works it into me, and I whimper as my cave walls stretch around him.

When he holds onto my hips and fucks me at a steady pace, a tremor of awareness runs through me. Brian is the one man I never dared allow myself to think about fucking. He's Sebastian's best friend, and we get together with him regularly. Of all my husband's friends, he is the most off-limits, and I fit around his cock like it was made for me. His cock is bigger than my husband's, and the curve of it massages the perfect spot deep inside. I'm going to climax quickly and there's no way to stop it. Oh fuck, now I'm going to be thinking about this every time I see him. It might have been better not knowing how well we fit together.

A strong slap on my ass breaks my thought process, and I buck my hips and cry out from the pain. Why am I being spanked? Brian speeds up the pace of his thrusts and spanks the other cheek. Ohhh, shit. I've never been one to crave being spanked, but somehow, with Brian, it feels natural. Yeah, this is dangerous.

Gripping the edge of the desk, I focus on the sensations swirling inside me. I'm still sensitive from my last orgasm, so I know there's no way I'll make it more than a few minutes without coming again. I grind my hips back into him, desperate for release.

"Fuck me harder," I beg, and he does.

Brian thrusts his hips faster and harder, and I throw my head back from the sheer joy his cock is creating inside me. I can feel the heat rising in my body as I prepare to come again. I squeeze tight around him and rotate my ass, wishing I could milk all his cum out of him. Originally, I wanted them to come on me, but now the idea of him filling me up sounds even better.

Brian groans and pounds into me harder. "Oh fuck, Jasmine, I'm gonna come."

I tense up, waiting for him to explode.

"Stop!" Sebastian growls.

Oh, shit. That's right. He can't come! At the very last second, Brian pulls out and stumbles away, cursing at himself for his lack of control.

Since Brian didn't actually come, Sebastian seems amused and chuckles, "That was a close one."

He gets out of his chair and stands behind me. Uh, is he going to fuck me in front of everyone? My body tenses up, expecting the head of his cock to probe my pussy at any second, but he slides his fingers inside me instead, and I relax.

"Just checking their work." His tone is jolly as he continues to rub me. "I need to be sure you're wet."

He can probably see the wetness on my thighs, so his excuse is flimsy. Not that I care. He can say whatever he wants if he works those clever fingers inside me some more. He caresses my clit with one hand while finger fucking me with the other, and the bliss builds again. My legs tremble as tension coils low in my belly, and all my muscles tighten as I edge towards release. Oh god, he better not stop.

I whimper as he presses hard on my clit and massages my inner walls with his fingers. My breath is ragged, and my eyes shut as I teeter on the brink of coming. Every part of me buzzes with joy as the intensity increases. I'm panting and mewling with each brush of his fingers as he plays my body as only he knows how from years of experience.

When he speeds up his finger fucking, I can't take it anymore and I come, screaming in delight as a soul-shattering orgasm robs me of my senses. The ecstasy continues to crest as he strokes his fingers into my pussy, and stars explode behind my eyelids.

"Ohhh fuck!" Another surge of pleasure rushes over me, and my brain melts. I can't tell where one peak ends and the next one starts, and the orgasm seems never ending as I ride his hand.

At some point I realize he removed his fingers, and my climax fades to soft aftershocks. Jesus, I don't know the last time I came that hard from just fingers, though I can't remember ever being this worked up. I'm so relaxed, I almost forget the other guys are in the room until one of them tugs me to a standing position and turns me around.

I gaze into Aaron's fierce expression, and my heart flutters with excitement. I don't know if I can come again, but it looks like he's not done with me. He picks me up and sets me on the edge of the desk and pushes my shoulders down.

He presses my knees towards my chest as I stare up at the ceiling. No one is asking permission or checking to see if I'm okay, and even though I know I can use Sebastian's and my safeword and all of this would stop, I don't want it to. I'm their sex doll tonight, and I welcome Aaron's meaty cock as he sinks into me again.

Since I still have my shoes on, I know this is probably quite the sight with me on the desk as a sexy dude fucks me. I try to picture it as if I was an outsider watching a porno. Shit, I wish we had this on video.

Aaron continues to plow into me, and when he presses my knees closer to my chest, my brain switches off again. I keep my eyes closed and drift in a daze of hedonism, unaware of anything but the all-over ripples of bliss. At some point, the other guys rotate in and replace Aaron, but I don't care who it is. No one cock is better than another anymore, and it's just continuous rapture.

I'm surprised when I realize no one is between my legs. It's over? I relax and look over at Sebastian, noting the adoration shining from him. My heart pounds, and I'm consumed with passion. I love this man with all of my heart. He's my "one," no matter how good the other cocks felt.

He walks over and holds me steady as he helps me stand up. My legs wobble in my heels, and I would have stumbled if he hadn't been supporting me. I wrap my arms around his waist and tip my head up for a kiss. He brushes his lips against mine, tenderly. Mmm, this is exactly what I need.

I'm still dazed, and murmur, "Thank you."

"You're welcome, love." He kisses me again, and I smile against his lips.

He pulls away from me and turns to the others. "Well, gentlemen, are you ready?"

They all nod while David states, "Oh yeah, I'm ready to come."

All the guys have their cocks out. Oh god, this is actually going to happen. I flush as I think about the vulgarity of what I'm about to do.

Sebastian steps aside and motions towards the floor. "Time for you to lie down and get your reward."

I'm vibrating with desire, and my mind goes blank as I catch David ogling me. He's rubbing himself slowly with pure lust radiating from him. Sebastian helps me kneel on the floor and I stretch out on my back, looking up at the men as they surround me and stroke their cocks.

"You're a beautiful woman," David groans as he tugs on his shaft faster.

A shiver of anticipation runs through me. I'm nervous and excited. Do I dare keep my eyes open? I watch, fascinated, as the guys moan, each one doing what he prefers. David beats his cock furiously, but Brian's hand moves with long and slow caresses. Leo's cock jerks in his fist, and Aaron's strokes are firm and purposeful.

"I'm going to come," David growls, and I watch his hand on his cock until I'm positive he's going to explode.

I close my eyes as he moans, and a splatter of wetness hits my face. David coming is the trigger for all the guys. A chorus of groans and grunts fills the air as their cum jets over my body. I imagine it's just a shower of cum, despite knowing it's probably only a few spurts each; fantasizing that I'm being coated in their seed is utterly filthy. As each drop lands on me, it reinforces the thought that I'm being painted in cum.

I'm lost in the debasement of the moment, and I don't realize they've stopped until I hear their clothes rustling as they put their cocks away.

Aaron says, "Fuck, Jasmine. That was wonderful."

I smile at all the men while they each thank me. I'm too dizzy to stand up, and I drift in a warm, happy place as the men talk in low voices. The office door opens and then shuts, and I feel a presence standing over me. I crack my eyes open. Sebastian and I are alone, and he's staring down at me with a glaze of desire.

"What now?" I ask, my voice barely a whisper.

He takes my hands, helping me get up. "You're a naughty girl, aren't you?"

I laugh and hold on to him so I don't collapse. "You think?"

"Yes, and you look delicious." He glances down at the cum coating my shoulders and chest, gathers some on his finger, and swirls it around my nipple. Oh fuck, that's hot. My breasts ache, and I wish he was sucking on my nipples.

He leads me over to the desk and picks me up, positioning me on the edge again. I spread my knees apart as he stands between them and fumbles with the zipper on his trousers. His hands are shaking, and it hits me that he desperately needs to fuck me. I brush his hands aside and ease Willy from his confinement. I almost giggle when his cock surges in my hand, already wet with pre-cum. Sebastian pulls me closer, trapping his erection against my stomach as he kisses me passionately.

My pussy hums the longer our tongues twirl together, and I moan into his mouth. This experience tonight was amazing, and I need his cock in me to feel complete. I'm the one who breaks off the kiss and I lean back on my elbows.

"Fuck me, Sebastian."

He grins as he positions his cock against my wet pussy. "Yes, babydoll."

With a single thrust, he's buried inside me, and I whimper in delight.

"That's it, Jasmine, take all of me."

He pulls out partway before plunging into me again. His thrusts are deep and hard, and I can tell he's not going to wait for me to come. He's a madman, pummeling into me, seeking release. His desire rekindles mine, and the pleasure builds in layers as I reel towards ecstasy.

As he bulldozes into me, slapping sounds fill the air. It's crazy how wet I am, but five guys toyed with me so I probably shouldn't be surprised. Sebastian's cock is familiar, and him driving into me with an animal fierceness is the perfect finale.

Hunger matches hunger as our bodies collide, and I realize that since none of the other guys came inside my pussy, it's only going to be Sebastian's cum dripping out of me on the way home. For some reason, that matters to me, and the thought of how he only allowed his seed inside me pushes me over the edge. I cry out and shudder from the force of my orgasm as liquid fire streams through my body.

"Oh fuck," Sebastian pants, grabbing my hips for leverage as he slams home repeatedly.

I cling to him as euphoria washes through me.

"I'm gonna come," he groans, thrusting wildly. "Oh, fuck, Jasmine…"

His words bring me back to reality, and I focus on matching his rhythm.

This time it's me making the demands. "Come for me."

"Yes. Yes, babydoll, yes!"

He shudders with release as his cum pours into me, sending aftershocks of bliss through my system as my heart races. I watch his face contort with pleasure while he pumps every last drop into my quivering pussy.

After a few moments, he slows down and holds still as he catches his breath. My heart rate evens out, and my breathing softens as he slips his cock out of me. When I sit up, he engulfs me in his arms and presses his forehead against mine.

"That was unbelievable," he whispers.

I snuggle into him and sigh happily. "I love you."

"I love you, too." He nuzzles my neck affectionately. "Are you ready to go home?"

"Um…" I look down between us, knowing I just got cum smears all over his clothes.

He laughs as if he's reading my mind. "Yeah, we're going to have to sneak out the back."

As he helps me off the desk, and retrieves my clothes from the floor, I'm struck again by how much I love my husband. We just did the filthiest thing I can ever imagine doing, and he's joking around afterwards.

I slip into my dress, and he zips me up. I smile softly, reminiscing about that first night in the bathroom with him. Thank God I was pretending to be a bimbo back then. He's the best thing that's ever happened to me.

Once I'm dressed, he entwines his fingers with mine. "Let's go, baby-doll."

I give his hand a squeeze and head with him towards the door. I'll follow this man anywhere.

The End

AUDITIONING THE BAND

CHAPTER 1

I scan the crowded dance floor, looking for my absent husband. Dammit, where did Gary go? He was here before I went to the restroom, but now I don't see him anywhere. I wasn't gone that long.

Today is not going how I wanted it to... at all. This is the second wedding we've attended this weekend. Normally I adore weddings, but this is eating up all my free time after several busy weeks. It's been twenty-one — no, now it's twenty-two days since Gary and I've had sex, and he promised me a weekend of pleasure. Fucking weekend of pleasure, my ass. We've been on the go non-stop since Friday afternoon. What in the hell does a woman have to do around here to get boned by her husband?

Sighing, I slowly circle the room, searching for Gary. It's not entirely his fault that it's been so long since we've had sex. I was sick one weekend, then he caught my cold and was sick the following one. Being an adult sucks sometimes, but not always in the good way, and this has been ridiculous. Gary swore he'd make it up to me this weekend. As the night continues, it's looking increasingly unlikely.

Last night I was a bridesmaid in my friend Vanessa's wedding, so I couldn't exactly ditch the wedding early. I couldn't even duck into a quiet corner for some well-deserved attention, since I had duties and shit to take care of. I was hoping for some aggressive cuddling once we got home, but we were both exhausted. The night ended in a soft snuggle pile with our two dogs in our king-size bed, which was good, but not what I wanted. I'm only a guest at the wedding tonight, which meant no responsibilities at the ceremony or before, but the day was eaten up by one monotonous chore after another until it was time to get ready.

I picked my dress carefully. Dammit, I was gonna get laid today, and I knew exactly what would get Gary going. I'm wearing a silky red halter-style dress that hugs my curves in all the right ways, a dress which he's nearly torn off me a time or five before.

My body's been expecting sex all day, and I got desperate enough to try and wheedle five minutes from Gary to just shove it in me and fuck me — anything to ease the ache between my legs. He said he wanted to wait until we had time for a proper fucking. That's my romantic husband for you. I'm not complaining about it, no way. I mean, like, oh no, my husband wants to wait until he can make me come. Poor me.

But Christ, can be it be this century please?

The wedding venue is beautiful, and the ceremony brought back memories of our nuptials. Gary squeezed my hand during the vows, which told me he was thinking of our wedding as well. Everything would have been perfect... if I wasn't so horny.

Once the ceremony ended, I excused myself to use the restroom and ran into my friend Jasmine. She's gorgeous, smart, and the type of woman I'd be insecure around if I didn't know her so well. She's down to earth and a hoot to hang out with, and I consider her my closest friend. When Jasmine told me her husband was using her on a freeuse day *and* he'd already used her multiple times that day, I couldn't stop the stab of jealousy. I tried to play it off like I wouldn't want to be used without coming. Yet I was the thirsty slut who tried to get my husband to do exactly that before the wedding.

Where is that man, anyway?

The wedding band ends the song they're playing, and the singer announces they are taking a break. As people clear the dance floor in search of refreshments, I finally spot Gary across the room. He's standing off to the side of the stage, talking to the singer. I should have figured he'd be with the band since the singer is his best friend, TJ.

What my loving husband doesn't know is I had a date with TJ before I met him. All we shared was a single kiss at the end of the evening, but it was memorable. TJ was young and idealistic and heading out on tour, hoping the band would hit it big. They never quite did, but the band is still together after all these years, through marriages, kids, and divorces. They mostly play weddings, but TJ is at our house often and he said he's happy with his life. And that's really all that matters, right?

He's still incredibly sexy — all sleek muscle on a powerful build. Better yet, both arms have full sleeve tattoos. This makes me wonder what other body art his clothes hide? In my daydreams I play find the tattoos, but it's his hands that rev my engine the most. He has long, thick fingers, and it's easy to imagine them stroking my most sensitive spots.

Yeah, this dude always set my panties on fire. Occasionally I still touch myself and fantasize about our date ending differently. What would have happened if I had invited him in for a nightcap? It's a harmless flight of fancy, and I'd never do anything with TJ. It doesn't stop me from rolling my hips and pushing my chest out as I approach the guys. When TJ catches my eye, the appreciative glint in his warms me. Yeah, I've still got it.

Gary's back is to me so he doesn't see me approach. When I sidle up to him and slide my arm around his waist, the conversation abruptly ends. I only caught a few sentences, but it sounds like they are making plans to do something together. Huh. I wonder what those two are up to? Focus. Gary. Bed. Soon.

Gary leans over to kiss my cheek. "Hey, hot stuff," he says, while TJ murmurs, "Hi Millie."

I give TJ a smile and a soft, "Hi," before playfully punching Gary on the arm and giving him a mock pout.

"I was looking for you everywhere. I thought you hooked up with some floozy and abandoned me."

I didn't really think that, but it's a game we play.

He winks at me, playing along. "You know I've only got eyes for you, babe."

"Damn straight. You're addicted to all of this."

When I run a hand down my hip, Gary laughs and pulls me closer to him. The corners of TJ's mouth quirk as he observes our banter. I've noticed TJ's usually watching me out of the corner of his eye when I'm around him. He's subtle about it, and it's flattering. It might be mean, but I hope he regrets not going for me all those years ago.

The guys pick up their conversation about an old buddy, and I listen for a few minutes before TJ excuses himself to take a break before the next set. Gary has a speculative look on his face as TJ leaves. I'm about to offer him a penny for his thoughts, but he speaks before I have a chance.

"TJ thinks I should take you home and fuck your brains out."

TJ is a good man. My opinion of him rises and I mentally take back my wishes of regret.

"I think you should listen to your best friend. He's obviously smart."

Gary faces me, pulls me against him and smirks. "He also thinks I'm crazy for not tapping your ass every chance I get."

Oh, fuck. That's filthy... and hot. My pussy buzzes and my panties grow damp. Were the guys drinking? There are no empty wineglasses anywhere and I didn't leave Gary alone long enough for him to get tipsy. Do they stand around objectifying me often?

Hell, maybe they do.

My nipples pebble, and I doubt the thin silky layers of my bra and dress hide it. Fuck, why can't I be more like Jasmine? I bet she'd look her husband straight in the face and tell him to use her whenever he wants. I can't get past the idea that getting turned on by my husband and his best friend talking about me like I'm a piece of ass to be used should be wrong. Yeah... I shouldn't like this, right?

My body has other ideas. I fight the urge to rub my thighs together. I don't want Gary to know this is turning me on. But that doesn't mean I can't have a little fun with this. He'll back down at some point.

I walk my fingers up his chest and neck. When I continue past his chin, he pretends to nip at my fingers. Yeah, my hubby is all talk and no action. He's my lovable teddy bear.

I keep my voice light. "So why aren't you? You had the chance earlier, and you didn't take it."

Gary shrugs casually. "I told him I'd rather watch him fuck you."

Oh jeez, as if. I don't bother to hold in my snort. "Why just TJ? Why don't I fuck the entire band?"

Hell, if we're going to play this game, let's play big.

He purses his lips, as if he's considering it. "I don't know. Is five guys too many in one night?"

"Five? There's only four in the band."

When he doesn't answer and captures my mouth for a panty-searing kiss, I melt into him.

Mmm, now this is more like it.

Our tongues twine together, and I press against him. Heh, he's hard. Someone's got a dirty mind and likes the thought of me fucking a bunch of guys. A pulse between my legs reminds me...

Oh yeah, it's me.

The longer the kiss lasts, the more I daydream about four guys kissing up and down my body at the same time. I've never admitted this to Gary, but it's one of my biggest fantasies. I'd love to be fucked by a bunch of guys at once.

I break off the kiss and push against his chest. "Hey, wait!"

"Hmmm?" He nibbles along the column of my neck, and I tip my head to give him better access. A shiver of delight almost distracts me and I lose my train of thought for a moment. What was I going to say? Oh, yeah!

"You never said..." I break off and moan as he sucks gently on my neck. Fuuuck, he's driving me crazy. All I want to do is straddle his leg and grind against his thigh until I explode. It's been so long since I've had an orgasm, it'll probably only take a couple of minutes.

He nips his way up to my ear and gently tugs on my earlobe with his lips. "What were you saying?"

Another shiver runs through me as his breath tickles the sensitive hairs on my ear. More wetness hits my panties. I shift from foot to foot, wishing we were alone. I'm close to not caring. I need to pull it together before he makes me so mindless that I beg him to fuck me in front of the entire reception.

"The band only has four people. Who's the fifth?"

He stops sucking on my earlobe and chuckles. "I'm the fifth."

Oh Jesus. He's so full of horseshit. He'd never watch me fuck the band, but I'm having fun with the fantasy. When he moves his hands behind me and cups my ass, pulling me closer to him, I sigh in pleasure. He seems to like our crazy talk as well.

"I could fuck them and take notes. Audition them."

He kneads my ass. "Yeah, keep a score sheet. Pass or fail."

"Mmm hmm," I moan. "I could be your freeuse slut that you're sharing for the night."

Gary's hand stills. Oh god, did I really say that?

He cups my ass again and his lips crush against mine. His tongue invades my mouth, setting off a sharp wild need deep in my core. Lust burns in my brain. If he screwed me on the stage right now, I'd ignore the crowd and beg for more. We need to go home... right fucking now.

We're both panting when the kiss ends, and he leans his forehead against mine. "Millie, what if I really want it?"

Holy shit balls, he's serious?

My body buzzes and I try to not squeal out a yes. I didn't dream this was a possibility. I never imagined he'd want to share me. My mind whirls with the implications, and I wish I could shut my brain off. For once in my life, can't I just go with the flow and enjoy it? Do I have to analyze everything?

I catch a whiff of his cologne and inhale deeply. He smells so damn good. It's a familiar scent that can relax or turn me on depending on my mood. Today it does both. I wrap my arms around his neck and squeeze him, enjoying our closeness after so many weeks of not feeling connected.

"Do you really want it?"

"Yes."

That simple response sends a thrill through me. Hot damn. A little voice in my head tries to tell me to slow down and think this through. I shove it aside. Not tonight, bitch.

I'm going to take what he's offering.

I give him a slow smile. "Today is a good day for me."

He studies my face for a moment before a lightness settles over his features. "I'll see what I can arrange."

CHAPTER 2

The rest of the wedding reception is a blur. When the band stops for the night, Gary leaves me sitting at a table while he talks to them. Knowing that he's asking them if they want to fuck me is vulgar... and awesome. I'm quivering thinking of it.

When he returns, he smiles mysteriously. "Everything is set."

What the fuck does that mean?

"So it's happening?"

His mouth pulls up at the corners again and for a second I think he won't answer me.

"Yes. My freeuse slut is getting shared tonight."

Ohhh, yes. My mind spins away into fantasies.

I know I'm not really a freeuse slut since this isn't how it works, but it's filthy to imagine I am. Gary could fuck me wherever he wanted, whether that was behind a potted plant in the lobby or underneath the emergency stairs. Heck, the entire band could rail me in the stairway and fill all my holes.

Are they all going to come in me?

I want one of them to blow their load on my face. I've never actually had that done before. Gary prefers my ass or pussy, though occasionally he fucks my tits and glazes my breasts. But never on my face...

I'm not sure how long I daydream about getting all my holes stuffed before Gary tips as head at me like he asked me something. My head spins and I stumble over my words.

"Sorry... what?"

He leans over and kisses my nose. "I asked if you were ready to be used."

"What, now?"

My eyes grow round. Um, where is this happening? I might fantasize about public sex, but I'm not actually into doing it.

"Yes, now. Do you trust me?"

His eyes glow with love and lust. Knowing he really wants this erases any remaining concern.

"Of course I do."

He kisses me softly. "Good girl. Now let's go get you ready. I want to see what you look like being spit-roasted."

Whoa, how long has he been thinking about this?

I try to visualize a guy in my mouth and one behind me, but I can't decide whether I want to suck on TJ or whether I'd rather he be the one fucking my pussy. Then again, maybe I can have both.

Shit, I need to focus. It takes a few moments for me to regain my composure.

"I'm ready."

We both rise. He takes my hand and pulls me towards a side door, walking fast in his eagerness. I rush to keep up. Where in the hell is he taking me?

The side door leads to an alley behind the venue. TJ's van, which they use to haul equipment, is parked close to the exit. As we approach, the back door swings open, revealing the four guys. My lips part and I suck in a breath.

I'm getting fucked in the van?

I've never seen the inside, so I peer closely. The walls are bare with angled brackets that would be good for gripping. A punch of lust hits me when I realize there's a thin mattress on the floor. They covered it with a red plaid blanket.

Uh, do they do this often? Is the blanket hiding a bunch of stains?

TJ must have noticed my expression. "We use it to protect the equipment, and if one of us wants to take a nap."

Uh-huh, likely story. Maybe they take horny MILFS to their van all the time after a wedding. Not that I'm one to judge. I mean, I'm here with them.

Their equipment is nowhere to be seen. Who's watching over the instruments?

Better yet, is this happening with the van doors open or closed?

Where is Gary going to be?

God, this is filthy. Jasmine isn't going to believe the night I'm having. I bet it rivals hers.

My swirling thoughts consume me and I almost don't hear TJ speak.

"Glad you could join us, Millie."

He's formal for how dirty this all is, and I hold in a giggle. The rest of the guys in the band all grin at me and I toss them a soft smile and a tiny wave. I've met them once before, but it was a couple of years ago and I don't remember their names. I don't want to admit I forgot, so I don't ask for an introduction. This makes it more vulgar anyway — getting fucked in a van in a dark alley by strangers.

Gary slides his hand in mine and gives it a light squeeze. "Are you sure you want this, Millie?"

I study him for a second, gauging how serious he is. His expression tells me he needs reassurance that I'm not doing this just for him. God, I love him with all my heart. This is a crazy, amazing step we're taking tonight, but I'm ready.

"Absolutely."

He glances at TJ and nods. "Go ahead."

TJ waves me in. "Let's get this party started."

I hesitate for a second before moving to the opening. Gary steps away and I climb into the cramped space. As soon as I'm inside, I abandon my shoes. I don't need them in here. The van is crowded with the mattress, me, and three other guys, so I kneel on the cold, hard floor. Yeah, the mattress is a good idea. My knees are going to be fucked up quickly without it.

The guitarist and bass player are sitting cross-legged, leaning against a bench-style passenger seat. The third band member, the drummer, is sitting sideways on the bench so he can watch the action. Every few seconds, his hand moves to his lips and I see him pop something bright orange into his mouth. I couldn't believe what I saw.

What the hell? Is he eating mellowcream pumpkin candy? Halloween was weeks ago. What sick fuck still has Halloween candy?

Gary opens the side door and climbs in to sit on the bench seat next to the candy-eating drummer. The guy offers Gary the bag. My husband doesn't even like that type of candy, yet he takes a piece. My mouth waters as I watch my husband chew for a moment. Those damn pumpkins are oddly addicting. Whenever I buy a bag, I can't put it down. But where's my offer of candy? I'm the one about to be fucked by multiple men. I need my strength.

Jesus. They just need some popcorn and then they'll be ready for the show.

I shift to ease the pressure on my knees, and I notice the floor of the van isn't that clean. Okay, maybe this wasn't the best idea. My dress is going to be a mess when we're finished.

TJ grins at me as he shuts the door, shrouding the car in semi-darkness. "We promised your husband you'll get multiple orgasms tonight. I hope you're ready for it."

Wow, Gary told them to make me come more than once? I glance at him and his eyes sparkle in the dim lighting. The floodlights in the alley illuminate the inside of the van so it's bright enough to see everyone, but the details are lost. The darkness makes me feel less like I'm on stage, more anonymous... and yet it also feels far more intimate than I expected.

TJ moves to the mattress and sits on it, then reaches his hand out to me. I take it and squeak when he pulls me into his lap. My ass nestles against the hardness in his pants, and he wraps his arms around me before giving me a quick kiss.

"This is what you wanted, right?"

Um... I dart a glance towards Gary and he's focused on us with a soft smile. Since Gary is still good, so am I. When I nod at TJ, his lips find mine again. I moan against his mouth as his hand moves to my chest, squeezing my breast. My nipples tighten in response and a pleasant buzz fills my mind. Mmm, I'm so ready for this.

TJ rubs his thumb across my hard nipple through the fabric of my dress, and I shiver. His body heat seeps into me, flooding me and bringing my passion to a boil. I wrap my arms around his neck, throwing myself deeper into the kiss. As our tongues war with one another, I wriggle in his lap, trying to get some relief for my aching pussy. The longer we kiss, the more difficult it gets to think.

I want to get lost in this moment.

When he breaks off the kiss, I blink several times to clear the lust haze. I peek over at the guys watching. All of them stare at me with hungry expressions, but Gary is the one I care about the most. The lines of his face are hard, and if I didn't know him so well, I would believe he wasn't happy.

But I do know him that well, and I smile inwardly. I'm looking into the face of my husband, who is so turned on that he's fighting for control.

My pulse accelerates. I'm going to get such a hard fucking when this is over.

CHAPTER 3

TJ kisses me again. This time, he slides a hand under my dress and between my legs. I spread them open as much as I can as he caresses the skin of my inner thigh. He keeps his other hand around me, holding me still while he explores. His touch is gentle, and I whimper when he reaches the damp fabric of my panties. The pair I'm wearing are just a wisp of lace and cover nothing.

Why did I even put them on? It would have been fun to tease Gary about not wearing any, and also have easy access for when I... get fucked in vans in seedy alleys.

His searching fingers push aside the fabric and slide into my folds. I moan as he lightly grazes my clit with two fingers. Oh god, his fingers are wonderful. He circles my clit with the perfect amount of pressure, and I buck into his hand, wanting more. Somehow, he knows exactly what I need.

TJ chuckles at my reaction and shifts his weight, putting more pressure against my ass with his hardness. My pussy clenches and I whimper louder. He slides his fingers into my pussy and I almost cry out from the pleasure.

TJ's voice is low and husky. "You're so wet."

Fuck. I need his cock inside me.

"Mmm," I moan as his fingers work magic inside me.

"I bet Gary's going to enjoy watching you come over and over again."

That's hot and I feel my need climb. Gary's nodding when I glance at him. I have zero problem with this plan, and I'm ready for him to watch me get fucked by all the guys.

I'm ready to be used.

TJ kisses me again, and I grab onto his shoulders. He alternates between stroking my clit and slipping his fingers inside me, curling them and stroking in an irresistible rhythm. I shudder and whimper, unable to stay quiet. He kisses me until I'm writhing in his lap and moaning so loud I'm afraid anyone walking past will hear me.

When it seems like TJ isn't going to go any further, I take matters into my hand.

Reaching behind my neck, I undo the halter straps on my dress and pull the top down, exposing my strapless bra. Since I'm sitting in his lap, it's difficult to maneuver. Instead of removing my bra, I push it down so my tits bounce free. TJ gives a low hum of satisfaction before taking over and moving his palm to cup my breast and tweak my nipple.

I glance at Gary to see how he's enjoying the show. He's smiling and watching intently. His eyes flicker to mine and I blow him a kiss that makes him smile. I think he approves of my exhibitionist tendencies.

TJ abruptly pushes me off his lap and I land on the mattress with a grunted "oomph." Since I'm on my back, chances are he's going to fuck me, and I gulp. My heart pounds. When he slides the bottom edge of my dress up to my waist, exposing my panties, I can tell shit's about to get real.

"So Millie, you husband told me earlier that you enjoy being called a dirty slut."

Whaaa... Gary told him that? My head spins when Gary laughs.

"Oh yeah, she loves it. The filthier, the better."

I look at Gary again, and he's grinning at me. This is the dirtiest thing I've ever done. Sharing it with Gary makes it better than anything I could have imagined. By comparison, a bit of dirty talk seems positively tame.

All of my attention is on Gary, so I jolt in surprise when TJ rips my panties off.

My brain freezes and I'm sucked into my deepest, darkest fantasy. I've never admitted it to anyone… the van… a dark alley… half clothed… a bunch of men…

Ohhh. Fuck.

My entire body lights up and I become hyperaware of every brush against my skin. My nipples pebble into hard diamonds, and I gasp when TJ tugs on them. I whimper in pleasure, and he continues until I'm biting my lip and squirming.

"Gary, you didn't tell me she likes it rough."

He slaps my tit hard and I moan.

"I didn't know." My husband's voice holds a hint of surprise.

I close my eyes, not wanting to look at him. I never told him because I knew he couldn't do rough. I married a cuddle bear who can fuck me hard, but he'd never get close to hurting me. My secret desires were too obscene to share with him.

TJ grabs my hips and rolls me onto my stomach as he kneels on the mattress beside me. He slips both hands under my stomach and lifts me up, pulling me onto my knees. I'm staring straight at the other band members and a zing of forbidden pleasure courses through me.

TJ slaps my ass hard enough to sting. "Spread your legs, Millie."

My pussy clenches and I gasp as wetness runs down my inner thigh. I position my knees apart, spreading my pussy wide open. I'm never this brazen, especially with someone I've never fucked before, let alone a van full of men, but fuck it. I'm way past caring about anything but getting a cock inside me.

His fingers run across the soft skin of my ass. Then his palm smacks my ass again, and I groan.

"Now, that's a dirty slut."

I clench my jaw to keep from crying out as TJ spanks me over and over. He smacks my ass harder each time before finally sliding his palm over my cheeks. He squeezes my globe firmly and I whimper, unable to stop myself.

I can barely think straight when TJ spreads my ass cheeks wide. His finger traces the crack of my ass down to my pussy, and I throw my head back in ecstasy when he thrust two fingers into me.

"Oh yeah, your slutty wife likes it rough," TJ says, and I mewl in response. "Can you handle it, Millie?"

Oh god. I'm going to come so fast when he fucks me, and I'm going to beg him to fuck me hard. This might be my only chance to fuck someone who can give me the roughness I crave and I want a taste of it.

"Yes, please, fuck me hard."

"Good slut."

His fingers move faster and I buck my hips into his hand, desperate to get his fingers as deep as they can go. I grip the mattress, panting for air. My pussy is sopping wet, and his fingers aren't enough. I sigh in relief when he removes his fingers.

Thank god. I'm finally going to get his cock.

As TJ moves behind me, I look at the other band members. Two men sit with their backs against the seat and both have bulging erections. One of them strokes himself through his pants. Everyone is staying silent, and I meet the gaze of each man briefly. Only the drummer smiles. The other two intensely focus on the action.

Oh god, this is so damn slutty.

TJ wrestles with his clothes for a moment, and when he grasps my hips, I lock onto Gary's gaze. As TJ teases my folds with the tip of his cock and coats himself with my wetness, I fight the urge to close my eyes. I need to be sure Gary is enjoying this.

Gary's face tells me everything. The wild look in his eyes says he's overcome with lust and just as excited as I am.

TJ's cock is larger than Gary's and I can feel him stretching me open as he penetrates me slowly. I moan when he bottoms out and holds still.

Fuuuck. Of course he'd have an enormous cock. I was already fantasizing about him, and this is going to make it worse.

He's not moving fast enough for me. The tension builds until I can't hold back any longer. I rotate my hips, forcing him to knock against me deep inside. Pings of pleasure radiate from my core. My toes curl as the bliss builds without him even moving.

TJ's laugh breaks the silence. "Seems your filthy slut is getting desperate."

"Please." I mewl in distress as he gives a couple of tiny thrusts.

"Please what?"

I need him to fuck me hard. I can get a soft fucking from my husband. My head spins and I close my eyes, sinking down into the depths of depravity.

"Fuck me... Fuck me rough. I need to be your filthy little fuckdoll that you use however you want."

I hear the other band members murmur as if my words surprise them. They probably didn't realize I'd debase myself if it led to a rough pounding.

I don't care what they think. The only person who matters is Gary.

I peek at him. Both his hands are on the back of the seat, gripping it tightly. I bet his cock is aching right now, and I smile softly at the thought.

TJ moves, pushing his hips forward and pulling back.

Oh, thank god.

I grind my ass towards him, moaning loudly as pleasure pulses through my veins. He plunges inside me and I lean down onto my elbows, opening so he can go deeper.

I lose all control when he slams into me, pistoning hard and fast. He's fucking me raw, and knowing that he's going to fill my pussy with his cum is nasty... yet I crave it. I want all the cum in me, no matter where I take it. They can fill all my holes and send me home with Gary a wet, dripping mess, and I'll love it.

TJ pulls out suddenly and I whimper in protest, but then he slams balls-deep inside me again. I cry out and arch my back, pushing against him as he fucks me hard.

"You're a good fuckdoll, taking what I give you."

I squeal in delight as the pleasure mounts. "Yes."

"Do you like knowing your husband is watching his slut get used?"

"God... yes."

And I really do. Gary and I never talked about me fucking anyone else, and I wouldn't agree to him doing the same thing. He's all mine. But this experience is only good because he's the one who asked for it.

"Gary, tell your slut you want her to come for you." He slows his movements and I whimper.

TJ slaps my ass, and I cry out. "Yes! Please let me come."

TJ slams his cock in and out of me, driving me closer and closer to the edge. He reaches around me to pinch my nipple hard and I howl from the intense, painful pleasure.

"Please, Gary. I need to come. Please!"

TJ grunts and his cock throbs inside me. I can tell his orgasm is building, and I desperately try to hold back my own. I squeeze my thighs together, trying to stave off my release until Gary says I can come.

"Please, Gary?" I sob, crazed and desperate.

I latch onto Gary's eyes, and he looks almost as lost as I am. Why isn't he saying anything?

TJ grunts as he hammers into me. "Tell your slut she can come."

The corners of Gary's mouth lift. "Come for me, Millie."

My body goes rigid at his words, and I scream as my climax tears through me. "Ohhhh, fuck!"

Convulsive waves grip me as TJ fucks me through my orgasm. When he comes, he grabs my hips, pulling me hard against him in a last thrust. He shouts out as he explodes, coating my cave walls with his warm cum. He spasms against me, unloading every drop before pulling out and collapsing onto his side.

TJ pants and I close my eyes, sinking further until my head is resting on my hands while his cum runs out of me. It's been years since I've had another guy inside me.

TJ's voice is hoarse. "Who's next?"

Two guys both say "me" at the same time. I keep my eyes closed, not caring who it is.

"Looks like you can fight over our slut." TJ moves away from me.

"We can share. I want to use her mouth." The guitar player has a deeper voice than the rest of them, so I know it's him speaking.

There it is. My husband's fantasy. He wanted to see me spit-roasted. I open my eyes as the bass player moves behind me, and the guitar player kneels in front of me, his cock already out.

"I hope you swallow. I'm going to fuck your mouth real good, and I've been told I'm quite a mouthful."

Oh, fuck. I thought I wanted a guy to come on my face, but now all I want to do is swallow a mouthful of cum.

He better taste good.

He's holding his cock in his hand, moving it towards my mouth. Dang, he's actually impressive. His cock isn't huge, but it's straight with prominent veins that I want to lick. He's going to be able to fuck my mouth easily.

This is going to be fun.

I almost forget the guy behind me until he seizes my hips and slams into me. The bliss spirals and I cry out.

"Ohhhh!"

The guitar player takes advantage of my open mouth and slides between my lips, cutting off my cries. I gurgle around his cock as he slides it all the way in. Every thrust from the guy behind me shoves me further on the cock in my mouth and it knocks against my throat. I've never done this before, and now I can't understand why not.

Goddamn, this is hot.

As I suck him, licking around his shaft, I taste his pre-cum and his musky male scent. I'm so worked up. Nothing bugs me, not even the full bush of hair at the base of his cock that tickles my nose. I just want them both to fuck me and fill me.

They continue like this, ping-ponging me between them. Delight ripples through my body. The guy fucking me hard from behind pushes into me with a smooth rhythm. I moan and whimper around the cock in my mouth, unable to keep quiet. The guitar player is blocking my view of Gary, and Gary better be able to see this. I want to hear how he felt while watching.

"Spank her." TJ calls out. "She likes it rough."

Oh, fuck. A sharp smack on my ass makes me moan. My pussy clenches around his cock.

The guitar player fucking my mouth slides his hands into my hair. He holds my head steady while he face fucks me a little rougher. He doesn't pull out, but keeps sliding in and out of my mouth. Damn, this is intense. I can feel myself getting close to coming again.

"Keep sucking, beautiful. You'll get your reward soon."

The impersonal nature of how they are using me and the dirty talk hits a kink I didn't know I had. I really feel like a fuckdoll.

Yeah, this is fucked up, and yet oh-so-wonderful.

A sharp spike of pleasure ripples down to my toes. I'm getting close. So very close. I wiggle my hips and push back into the guy fucking me while trying to take more of the guitarist's cock down my throat. The guitarist groans as my tongue swirls around his shaft and I suck him in deeper. I feel my core pulsing and relish the sensation for a moment before panic seizes me.

Oh no. No, no, this can't happen. I'm going to come. No one said I could!

Then all thought is erased. Bliss shoots through me, making me squirm, and I give a muffled cry as the ecstasy grips me a second time.

"Ohhh fuck!"

I buck and tremble as I'm assaulted by waves of pleasure. The guy in my mouth still holds my head as his thrusts turn short and quick. He pauses for a second before coming with a groan. The hot spray of his seed coats my throat and it seems never ending.

Damn, he wasn't lying. My throat works around him as I struggle to swallow, knowing it's futile.

The guy behind me howls as he bursts. For a blissful moment, I have two guys blowing their load inside me at the same time. My mind melts under the intensity of the pleasure. I can hardly breathe from the force of it.

When they're both done unloading, they pull out of me. Saliva and cum run down my chin and I wipe it off with my hand before collapsing onto the mattress. This is absolutely filthy.

I love it.

I close my eyes and drift, enjoying the intense relaxation from two orgasms as the guys move around the bus. I'm not paying attention until the drummer whispers close to my ear.

"Get up. We're not done with you."

Ohhhh, I forgot about him. I have one more band member to fuck.

I crack my eyes open and scramble onto my hands and knees as he gets behind me. Instead of slamming into me, as I'm expecting him to, he caresses my sore ass.

"Oh, you poor thing, you're all red."

I melt against him. This is nice. He can keep doing that as long as he wants.

"Now, be a good slut and move over to your husband and give him a little kiss like a good fucktoy."

What's this?

My eyes fly to Gary's. Oh shit, I haven't looked at him in a while. His glazed expression tells me he's so turned on he can hardly think.

The guys move out of my way as I crawl over to Gary. Leaning my arms on the bench, I'm face to face with him.

I give him a cutesy grin. "Hi, love."

He leans forward and brushes his lips against mine. "I love you, Millie."

"That's goooooood." My 'good' turns into a long moan as the drummer slides into my pussy.

My vision tilts and I grip the back of the seat as he jackhammers into me. Gary slides his hands to the sides of my face and kisses me deeply, swirling his tongue with mine as bliss zings straight to my fingers and toes.

I whimper into Gary's mouth as the drummer fucks me vigorously. I'm reeling with each thrust. Kissing Gary while another guy fucks me amps up the pleasure. Gary ravishes my mouth as we suck and taste each other. I'm beyond thinking of anything except coming again, and I'm spiraling higher and higher.

Gary pulls back from the kiss, and his eyes bore into mine.

"Come for me."

I nod frantically. "Yessss."

His eyes widen. I arch my back and scream as I come. My pussy clenches around the guy buried inside me, making him blow his load. He grunts as more cum floods me. He gives a few more thrusts as he empties his balls deep inside me.

When he pulls out, I collapse against my husband, gasping for air. Gary kisses me softly.

"You okay?"

I nod. "Yes."

Gary takes a corner of his shirt and wipes my face clean. I'm covered in sweat and cum, and I'm sure I look a mess. Gary and I exchange dopey grins as he moves his hand away from my face.

"There, all better."

One guy pulls my dress down and I glance over my shoulder. All the band members are smiling at me and I laugh at how satisfied they all look. Damn, I made a bunch of people happy tonight.

"Thank you guys. This was... an experience I won't forget."

A simple thanks doesn't seem adequate, but my head is too fuzzy to say more. Sitting back on my knees, I pull my bra up and adjust the top of my dress, tying it around my neck. TJ moves closer to me.

"Are you sure this was okay? I wasn't too rough?"

TJ's concern warms me. He's a good guy.

"Tonight was fabulous. It wasn't too rough."

"Good." He flashes a wicked grin. "Now tell Gary he better fuck you all you want, or else I'll come and take care of your needs instead."

I give a startled giggle as my pussy clenches. Oh, no. That's hot.

Gary just laughs, as if it's a big joke. "In your dreams, buddy."

TJ snickers with him. "A guy can hope."

The guys talk in low voices as I find my shoes, and TJ helps me out of the van. He squeezes my hand as Gary comes around the side to claim me.

"Thank you, Millie. Crazy night, huh?"

I murmur "Yeah" as Gary says his goodbyes and leads me to our car.

Oh Jesus. What did I just do?

CHAPTER 4

My thoughts whirl and I'm silent the entire car ride home. Is Gary really okay with this? I'm covered in four guys' cum. What if this ruins our marriage?

Gary keeps stealing glances at me, but doesn't speak. When we pull into the garage, he turns off the car and faces me.

"Are you really okay?"

I want to look away, but force myself to meet his eyes. "Yes. Are you?"

He cups my face and brushes my cheek with his thumb.

"I love you more than ever. You're my gorgeous goddess."

The love in his eyes soothes me, and I raise an eyebrow.

"You mean I'm a filthy slut who needs a shower?"

He laughs and kisses me.

"Yeah, but you're MY filthy slut."

I blow him a kiss as I get out of the car. He's behind me as we walk towards the door leading into the house. We're almost there when he grabs me and presses me against the wall of the garage.

"I think you forgot something."

Rubbing my body against his, I can tell his cock is rock hard. I decide to play dumb.

"Oh, yeah... I'd rate the band a 10 out of 10. Would do again!"

He barks out a laugh. "No, not that. But it's good to know."

I tease him some more. "Hmm… I don't think I forgot anything. Boy, am I tired."

I give a fake yawn that turns into a yelp as he uses a knee to spread my legs open. He yanks up my dress and fumbles with his pants, freeing his cock.

"You still have to fuck the fifth man."

I left my ruined panties in the van as a souvenir for the guys, so he's got free access to my pussy.

Gary bites my lip and kisses me deeply. He lifts my leg to wrap around his waist. "Time to remind you who you belong to."

He slams into me, making me cry out from pleasure. I clutch onto his shoulders as he pounds into me.

"Fuck, yes!"

He's like a madman, not caring about me coming. Shit, he must have been holding this in until he found out I was fine.

His hands dig into my hips as he bucks into me, fast and hard. I can hear the wet slap of skin on skin. He's fucking me so hard. I know I'll be sore tomorrow, especially after how many cocks I had tonight. He's knocking me against the wall with every thrust. Dang, he's never been this rough with me before.

It's awesome.

I hold on tight, enjoying the ride as my body quivers. Layers of pleasure build and tension coils low in my belly as every part of my body buzzes. Gary's flushed and puffing as he jackhammers into me.

Seeing his pleasure tips me over the edge. I catapult into a soul-shattering orgasm and I scream out his name as pleasure rockets me to a higher plane.

I'm so far gone, I don't know how much longer he fucks me. The waves of pleasure carry me until he groans and convulses, burying himself deep inside me. His ropes of warm cum bathe my insides as I come back to Earth. He slows his thrusts and leans against me, letting my leg slide down so I can stand on my own. He stands still, trying to catch his breath.

"Oh god, Millie. I love you."

Wrapping my arms around him, I snuggle as close as I can get. "I love you too."

A cough from the end of the garage startles us both. Oh fuck, he forgot to close the garage door. No one is visible, but the manly voice of our neighbor calls out from the side of the house.

"I saw you guys get home and wanted to return your casserole dish. I'm leaving it out here. You guys have a good night!"

Gary looks at me with round eyes, and I feel the heat of a blush creep up my face. My stomach clenches.

Oh, my God. How am I going to face the neighbor ever again? How much did he hear? And why didn't he wait until morning to return our dish? Dammit!

Gary's loud laugh brings me out of my panic. "Come on, love. Let's get cleaned up and go to bed. You know he's walking home and wishing he could fuck Jennifer against the garage wall."

I grin back at him. Jennifer is a good friend of mine. Maybe I should ask her later if she got unexpectedly railed tonight. If so, I'll tell her she can thank me.

I slide my hand into Gary's. "Let's go. If you're lucky, I'll let you soap me up in the shower."

"Hah, if I'm lucky?"

I give him a saucy grin. "Yeah, I heard you have to do anything I want, or else TJ is going to come over and service me."

Gary grumbles behind me, "He said I had to fuck you, not do anything." I hold back my laugh.

Oh yeah, this is going to be fun.

My pussy hums to life, and I try to push back any thoughts about TJ really coming over to service me.

Yeah... I'm such a slut.

And it's glorious.

The End

Acknowledgments

This bundle took a village to come together, more so than anything I've written before. Thank you to the following people.

Steph Brothers - I absolutely LOVE the covers you helped me with for this series. You're amazing.

Wordcat - Thank you, like always, for your editing help with the first four stories. I hope you know how much I value everything you do.

Adam Gaffen - Thank you for editing Auditioning the Band. I really appreciate having multiple options for a great editor.

Hanna from Green Proofreads - Thank you for giving this a last proof for the bundle.

Kristin Lance - Thank you for listening to my ideas and helping me when I was stuck. You're a wonderful friend.

My various beta readers (I might have forgotten everyone who helped by now) - Alec Lake and Anya Knightly, for sure. My Patreon people, when I had one, for giving me the feedback on Taking Them All that prompted me to keep writing more to the story.

ABOUT LACEY CROSS

I'm mainly a writer who got bored during the pandemic and turned to erotica out of desperation. I found out I love the creativity and challenge of self-publishing sexy stories. I write a variety of kinks, but most are wife sharing with a touch of BDSM power control.

Connect with me at:

https://lacey-cross.com/